"Why did you do that?" Faith stepped back, wishing she wasn't shaking, wishing she didn't want to beg him to kiss her again.

"You needed to be kissed."

If Vale thought his hot kisses had left her any less in need of being kissed, he was wrong.

All he'd managed to do was show her what she'd been missing—what she now knew she desperately wanted.

Determined to salvage her pride, she frowned, wishing he wasn't still touching her. "Says who?"

He rubbed his thumb across her lower lip. "Says me."

A shiver whipped through her body, prickling her flesh. "Even if I did need to be kissed, that's not your place. I told you on the day I agreed to this trip with you—I won't be lumped into the category of one of your girls."

He seemed to consider her comment a moment. "You're wrong, Faith. Kissing you is exactly my place. This weekend you *are* my girl."

Dear Reader

Lighthouses fascinate me. Everything about them—the way they look, their purpose, their history—all of it. However, I'd never actually seen one until I was researching for this story.

During a visit with a dear friend, we and our two full-of-personality daughters drove to the Cape May lighthouse. I remember feeling giddy at my first glimpse, and was just wowed when I was actually standing at the top, leaning against the railing, looking out over the horizon.

Like me, geeky Dr Faith Fogarty has never seen a lighthouse—not until she spends a high society weekend away from reality with hunky Dr Vale Wakefield. Faith has been enamoured of her brilliant playboy boss since before they even met in person. But while in Cape May she discovers a whole new side to herself—one she embraces. And, like the lighthouse they visit, she lets her inner light shine in the hope that Vale will find his way to her and to her miniature poodle Yoda.

Vale and Faith pass two women and their giggly daughters in the stairwell. Well, I won't say who they are, but I'm betting you can guess. I hope you enjoy Vale and Faith's Cape May adventure as much as I did my visit there and writing their story.

Happy reading!

Janice

FLIRTING WITH THE SOCIETY DOCTOR

BY
JANICE LYNN

First published in Great Britain 2011
by Mills & Boon, an imprint of Harlequin (UK) Limited.
Large Print edition 2011
Harlequin (UK) Limited, Eton House,
18-24 Paradise Road, Richmond, Surrey TW9 1SR

© Janice Lynn 2011

ISBN: 978 0 263 21776 6

Harlequin (UK) policy is to use papers that are
natural, renewable and recyclable products and made
from wood grown in sustainable forests. The logging
and manufacturing process conform to the legal
environmental regulations of the country of origin.

Printed and bound in Great Britain
by CPI Antony Rowe, Chippenham, Wiltshire

Janice Lynn has a Masters in Nursing from Vanderbilt University, and works as a nurse practitioner in a family practice. She lives in the southern United States with her husband, their four children, their Jack Russell—appropriately named Trouble—and a lot of unnamed dust bunnies that have moved in since she started her writing career. To find out more about Janice and her writing visit www.janicelynn.com

Janice Lynn won
THE NATIONAL READERS' CHOICE AWARD
for her first book
THE DOCTOR'S PREGNANCY BOMBSHELL

To my dear writing pal, Kathleen Long.
Thank you for your unfailing friendship and
belief in me, all the late-night hotel room
giggles at writer conferences, and for giving
me my first glimpse of a lighthouse.
Love you!

And to Abby Lynn and Annie Long,
since Abby says this book has to be
dedicated to them, too, since they helped
with the Cape May research. ☺

CHAPTER ONE

"No way am I going to a wedding with you."
Faith Fogarty shook her head, knowing this time
her boss had pushed her too far. "Uh-uh, no way.
I won't be lumped into the category as one of
your girls."

Glad no one seemed to be paying them the
slightest attention, probably because their co-
workers were all trying to look busy so as not to
attract the boss's attention, Faith retreated into
the privacy of Dr. Vale Wakefield's office, him
hot on her heels.

"I'm not asking you to be one of my girls," he
pointed out, unnecessarily.

Of course he wasn't asking her to be one of
his girls. She wasn't his type. She had a brain.

"I'm asking you to accompany me to a family
gathering where I will be tortured mercilessly
by my family if I don't bring a date. They'll try

and hook me up with every single female there."
He made a gagging sound.

Having no sympathy whatsoever for one of
New York City's most sought-after eligible
bachelors and top-notch neurosurgeons, Faith
shrugged. "So take Lulu."

Lulu was the willowy blonde who'd accom-
panied Vale to a big charity ball the previous
Saturday night. Faith had read about the event,
seen a photo of the model plastered to Vale's side
in the society section of the Sunday paper. An
entire column had been dedicated to whether
or not the exotic model would be able to get the
Wakefield heir to the altar. Faith had wadded up
the paper and tossed it in the trash, where such
gossip belonged. Of course Vale wouldn't marry
that woman.

"To quote you, 'Uh-uh, no way.'" Vale empha-
sized each word. "Do you have any idea what
type of problems I'd create if I brought Lulu or
any woman with me to a family gathering, much
less to a wedding?" He shuddered with all the
drama of a person who'd just bit into the bitter-
est dish. "She'd be hearing wedding bells long

before we got to the ceremony. There is absolutely no way I'd take a *real* date to my cousin's wedding." His intense blue eyes narrowed with the steely purpose that put most in a tizzy. "I'm taking you."

And that was where Faith fit into Vale's life.

Not a real date. Not someone he would consider dating or bringing to a New York City charity ball. Not someone he would consider loving or having a real relationship with. Not that any of Vale's relationships were real, not unless no-strings-attached sex counted.

He'd pretty much just admitted that he didn't even see her as a woman. Great. She was a sexless brain.

Sucking in a deep breath, she shook her head. "No, thanks. Accompanying you to family functions is not in my job description."

He grinned the devilish smile that had her heart thumping overtime whenever he flashed his pearly whites. "I could have my attorney add an addendum to your contract."

"Forget it." She narrowed her gaze in as menacing a glare as she could pull off when he grinned at her that way. Why couldn't she be immune to him? After all, he was a bra-size before brain-size typical male. "I'm not going to a wedding with you."

"I'd pay you."

As if that made one iota of difference. As a neurologist specializing in Parkinson's disease, she earned a good salary from her job. A job that didn't require her fending Vale off from wannabe bridezillas and well-intentioned family members.

He named a figure that made her head spin.

"No." Fighting to keep her composure, she picked up a stack of consult requests from the long mahogany table that occupied one side of the expansive room that served as his office. One by one, she flipped through them, sorting out the more urgent cases that she wanted to discuss as possible surgical candidates with Vale.

He crossed the room, standing so close that if she'd turned toward him she'd likely bump him. She wouldn't look, wouldn't turn, but would he please quit staring at her?

"You might as well concede, Faith." He put

his hand on her shoulder, eliciting a thousand tiny shivers that caused tremors all the way to her very core. "In the long run I always get what I want."

He was right. He did always get what he wanted. With women. In life. Vale Wakefield led a gilded life. One where he'd been blessed with money, looks, intelligence, gifted surgical hands, and that something more that just made him impossible not to like. Women wanted him. Men wanted to be him. Little old ladies made him cookies and cakes, for heaven's sake.

At work she could maintain distance, keep her unwanted attraction to him safely tucked away, but at a wedding? Would he take one look at her and realize she dreamed of being the one he danced with at ballroom charities? The one warming his bed?

A *wedding*.

Not even for Vale would she face another wedding.

She was not going to give in. He did not have to get his way with her every time he crooked his finger. This time he'd passed the limits of her endurance.

"What I want is for you to come with me to my mother's this weekend and accompany me to Sharon's wedding."

Faith dropped the consults onto the table, turned to face him, anger sparking deep in her chest. Why did he just assume that she was at his beck and call 24/7? "Did it ever occur to you that I might already have plans for this weekend? That I might have a life outside work?"

Rarely was Vale caught off guard. Even more rarely did he show shock when someone actually did surprise him. But the darkening of his pupils gave clue to the fact that he truly had never given any thought that she might not live every moment in hopes of him deigning to ask her to work late, to come in over the weekend to review an important surgery case, to drop everything and go to his cousin's wedding with only four days' notice.

Of course, he hadn't given any thought to her potential plans. Why would he? He didn't find her attractive and apparently couldn't imagine anyone else doing so. Why wouldn't she be available at his every whim?

Which hit a bit too close to home.

Faith's teeth ground together. Sure, she wasn't glamorous like the women he dated. She couldn't be even if she tried. Not with her stick-straight dishwater blond hair, plain green eyes, and too big mouth. Still, his split-second shock at the possibility that someone might want to spend time with her for non-work purposes hurt. Hurt so deeply that had she put her hand to her chest to find her life blood seeping out, it wouldn't have surprised her.

Because whether she'd wanted to or not, she'd fallen head over heels in lust with Vale the day she'd come to work for him eighteen months ago.

Eighteen months of the sweetest mix of pleasure and pain at working so closely with him and him never seeing her as anything more than a neurologist who shared his passion for finding a cure for Parkinson's disease. Which was for the best, really, since a one-night stand, which was all he ever seemed to do, would only destroy her career with Wakefield and Fishe Neurology, Inc.

"This isn't up for debate. I'm not going to your cousin's wedding." She really wished he wasn't standing so close. So close she could make out the darker blue rim surrounding his vivid eyes, so close she could smell the musky scent of his aftershave, so close she could press her body to his with only a step forward.

Gee, if she stripped naked, would he even notice she was a woman? Or would he just frown, tell her to get dressed, they had more brain mapping to do? That her attraction to him was simply her olfactory mucosa sensing the overly abundant androgens he emitted, causing her cortisol levels to skyrocket, and that was why she wanted to lean in and press her lips to his throat?

"You already have plans this weekend?" he pushed. Just as she should have known he would. The spoiled little rich boy in him couldn't stand to lose, not get his way. Her fate had been sealed before the conversation had started.

"Somewhere you are supposed to be that you can't attend with me?" His eyes pierced her, seeming to know the truth without her having to answer.

She wanted to lie, wanted to say that some gorgeous man was anxiously awaiting Friday evening so he could whisk her off her feet, wine her, dine her, *make her cortisol level go through the roof*, and show her the time of her life.

"I don't have specific plans—" unless cleaning her apartment and walking Yoda, her miniature poodle, counted "—but that isn't the point."

His expression brightened. "Of course it's the point. You don't have specific plans. I need you to accompany me to Cape May. We'll review the latest data from Brainiac Codex while we're there and make the weekend a working one so it won't be an entire lost cause. It'll be perfect."

"No, it won't be perfect. I do not want to go with you to a wedding in Southern New Jersey." Neither did she want to spend her weekend reviewing the computerized brain-mapping research they were conducting. Yes, she loved her job, but she'd actually thought that with him out of town for the weekend she'd have some time to herself for once.

Why was she bothering to argue with him? Why did she think she could dissuade him when he'd set his mind to something? No one could, least of all her.

Still, she stubbornly held on to her pride. "No. No. No."

"Don't you like weddings?" Creases marred his forehead. "What am I saying?" He shook his head as if to clear his thoughts. "All women like weddings."

Maybe in his world, but not hers.

"Not this woman."

His brow lifted and she knew she'd said the wrong thing, revealed too much. Stubborn was one thing, stupid quite another.

"Why not?" he asked, as if she'd tell him about just how many weddings she'd been to as her mother's maid of honor. Obviously one too many as just the thought of going to another made her histamine concentration double. Any moment she'd break out in hives. She scratched an already itchy spot on her neck.

"I just don't." No matter how much he pried, she wasn't going to tell him more.

He studied her a moment, then dismissed her comment as too inconsequential to be taken seriously when in opposition to his wishes.

"You'll like this one," he assured her. "My cousin Sharon never does anything halfway, and she's marrying the Philadelphia Eagles' quarterback. You'll have fun."

"Sure, I will. That's why you're so excited about going. Because of how much fun you'll have." Faith sighed. He wasn't going to be dissuaded. Wasn't going to let her off the hook. Whether she wanted to or not, she was going to be spending the weekend at Vale's family's beach house in Cape May, a couple hours' drive south of the city. As his date to his media darling cousin's wedding. The paparazzi loved Sharon Wakefield and the former beauty queen was never far from the press's spotlight.

"Okay, you're right." He grinned at his admission. "Weddings aren't my thing, but Sharon is my favorite cousin and I'm in the wedding party. It isn't as if I can send an exorbitant gift and beg out of this one."

"Like you usually do with family and friends'

get-togethers?" He was in the wedding party? Although the media knew of the upcoming nuptials, the exact details were very hush-hush. Faith hadn't realized when she'd heard Vale mention his cousin's wedding to the famous football player that he'd be wearing a tuxedo and standing near the alter. Experiencing Vale in a tuxedo was quite possibly worth whatever heartache she'd suffer at attending yet another wedding that would only serve to remind her that nothing was for ever despite promises made.

He waggled his dark brows. "You'd better believe it."

"Fine, I'll go." It wasn't as if he'd give her a choice when all was said and done. He'd be like a dog with a bone and gnaw away at her protective covering until he sank his teeth into her vulnerable center.

His perfect mouth curved into a devilish smile. "I knew you would."

He could have at least sounded surprised, not quite so cocksure. Then again, that was Vale. Always confident. Always sure. Always a winner.

"Let's start going through these." She motioned to the latest data on their brain-mapping research that would hopefully lead the way to new treatment modalities for neurological disorders. "I've got to be in clinic at nine."

Twenty minutes later, Vale leaned back in his chair, staring across the table at the godsend he'd hired based solely on gut instinct a year and a half ago. There hadn't been an actual opening for another neurologist at Wakefield and Fishe Neurology, but quite frankly the young woman who'd finagled an appointment with him had impressed the hell out of him.

He'd learned long ago after a few eye-opening experiences to trust his gut and his gut had said not to let this one go. He'd hired her on the spot.

Even now he could hear her stunned "Don't you want to check my references first?"

He'd stared straight into her big sparkly eyes that made him think of the green apple hard candy he'd loved as a boy. Her dull framed glasses couldn't hide their appeal or their honesty. The ugly frames still didn't.

He'd never regretted his decision that day.

Faith was more like his right-hand man…er… woman. When he'd been awarded a grant to do research on Parkinson's, which involved the surgical implantation of an innovative two-lead device that emitted electrical impulses at the brain stem, he'd immediately convinced Faith to come on board. In the office and with his research they were a team. Working as many hours as he did, she never disappointed him, often pointing out fresh angles to cases, looking at the facts with intelligence and with an out-of-the-box canniness that almost matched his own. More and more he relied on her insight, on her thoughts as to the best way to approach each patient.

Now he was relying on her to bail him out of an uncomfortable situation with his family. During last night's call from his mother, letting him know just how many single females were going to be in attendance and were looking forward to meeting him, he'd immediately put a stop to her matchmaking by announcing Faith would be coming to the wedding with him.

He probably should have asked her first, but she'd never balked at any request to work late or over the weekend. True, spending the weekend at his mother's beach house wasn't exactly the same thing as working late.

Still, her comment about possibly having plans intrigued him in ways he couldn't explain. Just what did Faith do in her free time?

"Do you have a boyfriend?"

She glanced up, staring wide-eyed at him with an open mouth. "What does me having a boyfriend have to do with anything?"

"If there's someone special in your life, he might take exception to us spending the weekend together. I'd be happy to reassure him your virtue is safe with me."

Faith chewed on her lower lip, staring at him as if trying to decide on the right answer.

A flutter started in Vale's chest, one similar to that he felt in surgery when encountering something imaging scans hadn't picked up on. Was there someone warming his employee's bed? Someone she went home to night after night complaining about her slave driver of a boss?

Why did the thought of anyone touching her bother him?

Her eyes sparked green fire and her chin lifted, as if his question had offended her. "Whether or not there is someone special in my life, I am quite capable of keeping my personal life in order, Dr. Wakefield, and of assuring any man of mine that he has nothing to fear where *you* are concerned."

Vale bit back a grin. His ever-efficient neurologist had just put him in his place. "I didn't mean to upset you, Faith. Sometimes I forget not everyone is as dedicated to their career as I am."

Her lips pursed. "You've never had cause to question my dedication to my job."

"True. Which is why you're coming with me this weekend. I'll have Kay send you the itinerary for the weekend so you'll know how to pack."

How had Thursday evening arrived and Faith still hadn't found time to go shopping for a new outfit? Of course, she knew how. For exactly the same reason she currently wasn't shopping.

Because she was working. Vale had seemed intent on occupying every second of her time this week. Worse than normal. To keep her from having time to come up with an excuse not to accompany him this weekend?

She, Vale, two neurosurgeons, two neurophysiologists, and a couple of research assistants working on the Parkinson project were spread out around the twenty-seat cherry table at one end of Vale's office. Despite the long hours they'd put in every night that week, they'd barely made a dent in the pile of work to be done before they tested the hypothesis in the operating room. Although deep-brain stimulation therapies had been in use for years, with the new data from the Brainiac Codex, the hope was that the new device would relieve the tremor associated with Parkinson's. If successful, great strides in the treatment of the debilitating disease would be made.

She wiped her hand across her face.

"Something wrong?" Vale leaned in and whispered next to her ear, his warm breath making the tiny hairs on her nape stand at attention.

She glanced his way, wondering where he drew his boundless energy from, wondering how nothing ever fazed him or made him lose his infamous control. He'd work all day, most of the night, and still have photos of himself and some beauty queen appear in the papers when he'd hit a late-night club or fancy restaurant.

"Nothing a good night's sleep won't solve." True. She hadn't slept well since he'd told her she was going to Cape May. Plus, no way was she going to tell him that her mind was wandering from the data they were poring over to thinking about what she was going to wear at his cousin's wedding. No way would she risk losing the respect she'd fought so hard to gain.

Unfortunately, he didn't look convinced by her answer, studying her with eyes too intelligent for his own good. "You're sure?"

"Yes, I'm sure." She glanced at her watch. A little after seven. If they finished up within the next hour, maybe she could swing by a dress shop and pick up something new to lift her confidence at spending the weekend with Vale's glitzy family. She looked around at the room full of researchers who were settled in for the long haul and bit back a sigh.

"Got a hot date?"

"What?"

He'd spoken low, for her ears only, but her response came out as a squeak that had several pairs of eyes glancing their way and just as quickly going back to their work.

"That's the third time in the past fifteen minutes you've looked at your watch," he pointed out. "We must be keeping you from something important."

Again Vale spoke low, but Faith's ears burned. Was everyone trying to look as if they were ignoring them or were they truly so absorbed in their work? Marcus Fishe was the only one whose gaze lingered on them. Faith quickly looked away from Vale's partner's curious eyes. Although Marcus's focus within the clinic was geared more toward issues with multiple sclerosis, he'd jumped on board with the Parkinson's project in the hope that the brain-mapping data would lend itself to other treatments.

"My work is important." Determined to keep her mind absorbed on her work and not on the fact she'd be spending her weekend with Vale, Faith highlighted an abnormal signal recording from the basal ganglia to the motor cortex on the patient profile. "I've still got to pack for this weekend, and I'd hoped to… Never mind."

There was no reason to tell him she'd hoped to go shopping, to spend time with Yoda, to have a break from Vale to recharge herself prior to attending the wedding.

Setting his ink pen down, he continued to study her in a way that made her feel as if she'd grown an extra nose on her face. "You did get the itinerary from Kay?"

"Yes, your head nurse slash assistant is as efficient as ever." She liked Kay, thought her brighter than many of the clinic's more educated personnel, including a few of the neurologists and surgeons. "The itinerary seems standard. Rehearsal tomorrow night followed by dinner, Saturday pre-wedding activities, the wedding ceremony, and then the reception with champagne, dancing, and a romantic sunset at the beach."

He snorted. "I'll warn you not to be fooled. There's nothing standard about my family."

"I wouldn't expect otherwise."

Vale rarely spoke of his family but it was impossible not to know about them as they were constantly in the press. His cousin Sharon had won Miss Pennsylvania a few years back, had gained notoriety when she'd posed topless for an exorbitant amount of money that she had then handed over to the New York City Widows and Orphans of Firefighters Fund, and had then been promptly de-crowned. Another cousin was a congressman. Another a senator. Vale's mother headed so many charities it was impossible for Faith to recall them all. His father had built a real estate empire prior to his death in Vale's teens. Apparently all Wakefields were over-achievers, the one grinning at her no exception.

"Oh?" His eyes glittered with amusement. "What do you expect?"

Her and her big mouth.

"I just meant that you're a highly successful man with good genes," she whispered, casting a leery glance around the quiet group at the table. Yet again, Marcus was watching them. Great. She glared at Vale. "Surely that trait must run in the family?"

"I'll let you decide for yourself tomorrow night." Leaning close, he flashed a wickedly dangerous smile. "I have good genes?"

She rolled her eyes. "You don't need me to answer that. You know you do."

"Right." His grin widened.

Face burning, ears roaring, Faith resumed an intent study of the brain wave data she held, resisting the urge to glance at her watch again or to sneak a peek at the man sitting next to her. She could feel his gaze searing into her with the power of hot metal slicing into butter.

Two hours and several cups of coffee later, Faith rotated her neck, trying to work out the crick that had developed while studying the last patient profile for some missed detail, as they narrowed their choices on who met their study criteria for surgical implantation of the device.

So much for her shopping trip before heading home. And poor Yoda. Another late night with Mrs. Beasley. Before long her baby was going to think he lived at the elderly neighbor's apartment rather than with Faith. Especially as the cream-colored poodle would be spending the weekend in Mrs. Beasley's care, too.

Much later, Vale pushed the stack of patient brain-mapping profiles away from him, surprising her since they'd not made it through the rest of the stack. Although all of the others had left a little after nine, she'd already surmised she and Vale wouldn't leave before midnight.

"I've had enough." He stretched his arms above his head, drawing her gaze to how his shirt pulled taut over his chest.

She quickly glanced away, looked down at her watch. Maybe she'd have time to shop yet.

She sighed.

Maybe not.

The nicer dress boutiques would all be closed. Great.

She'd just wear the black cocktail dress she'd bought for last year's Christmas party. She wasn't crazy about the idea of wearing black to a wedding, but with its skirt flared at the hem the dress would do in a pinch and was the closest thing she had to appropriate wear for media darling Sharon Wakefield's glamorous wedding. As far as the reception, she'd make do with whatever she could find in her rather boring closet.

"Will he still be waiting?"

She blinked at Vale. "Who?"

His blue eyes darkened. "Whoever I've kept you from."

He almost sounded as if he'd intentionally kept her at the office. Actually, when the others had left and she'd started to stand, he had asked her opinion on a patient report he'd just read, ensuring she'd stay on to read the profile.

Had he intentionally kept her there? What possible reason would he have for doing so?

She took a deep breath, telling herself she was tired, imagining things, but for once gave her boss a flippant answer. "Regardless of how late you keep me, he's always glad to see me."

She wasn't lying. Not really. But, seriously,

she expected Yoda not to know who she was if she didn't start spending more time with him. Thank goodness for their nightly snuggles and early morning walks.

"Maybe you should go ahead," he suggested, his dark eyes unreadable. "I'll finish these."

He was staying? Telling her to go on? Was he testing her? Seeing how dedicated she was to her career?

"When you said we should call it a night, I thought you meant both of us. I don't like the thought of leaving you here alone."

Leaning back in his chair, he laughed. "Do you think I can't take care of myself?"

No matter how she tried she couldn't keep her gaze from lowering, from tracing over the strong lines of his neck, over the tanned V of skin exposed where he'd removed his tie and unbuttoned the top couple of buttons, down his broad shoulders that his tailored shirt accented, down his forearms bared where he'd rolled up his sleeves. And his hands.

Lord, how she loved his talented hands.

Tanned, strong, long-fingered, ring-free. She

particularly liked that last part, although eventually he'd marry one of the beauties he bedded. Then what? Would she be able to continue working with him, knowing how she dreamt about him, knowing he belonged to someone else?

That question was one that crept into her mind from time to time, filling her with panic, filling her with the dreaded knowledge that some day she might leave Wakefield and Fishe.

She lifted her gaze back to his, was startled to look into smoky blue eyes filled with awareness.

Awareness that she'd looked at him not as his employee, not as a fellow physician, but as a woman with real needs.

What was wrong with her?

She swallowed, trying to clear her throat, trying to buy herself time while she racked her brain for something to say that would defuse the situation.

Only, she didn't know what to say.

Regardless of how much his awareness scared her professionally, as a woman, the flicker of interest in his eyes set light to a hope that threatened to consume her very soul.

CHAPTER TWO

VALE finished his cellphone conversation with his cousin Sharon and turned toward Faith. They'd just left the hospital following a globus pallidus DBS implantation, and were walking back to Wakefield Tower, where Wakefield and Fishe occupied the entire fifty-sixth floor.

Vale was enjoying the late spring air, enjoying the hustle and bustle of the busy New York sidewalk, people from all walks of life rushing past him and Faith. Numerous vendors lined the streets, selling everything from designer sunglasses to cheap "I Love New York" T-shirts. A hot-dog street vendor called out to someone and Vale's stomach growled in response.

"Let's grab an early lunch before heading back," he suggested. Quite often they'd pop into a restaurant or grab take-out so they could review a case while dining. Working with Faith made lunch more enjoyable. "Subs or Chinese?"

"Neither." Not a single hair out of place on her tightly pulled-back hairstyle, Faith shook her head. "I can't do lunch today."

Mentally, he ran through her schedule. They were leaving the office early to head to Cape May so she only had a few afternoon appointments. "You aren't scheduled for anything until one, are you?"

She didn't meet his eyes. "No, but I have other lunch plans. Sorry."

Vale's gut tightened. Had she made plans to meet the mysterious man in her life? The one who'd been glad to see her the night before even though Vale had managed to keep her out past eleven? Had she lain in his arms recounting the day's events?

How had he not known she was seeing someone? Why did the fact that she was make his stomach knot?

Not because when she'd looked at him last night, he'd grown hard in response to her visual undressing. She'd liked what she'd seen and hell if he hadn't wanted to preen under the intensity of her green gaze.

Which was all wrong. He never, ever got involved with a colleague, and particularly not one who worked for him.

Besides, she wasn't his type.

Sex with Faith would be complicated, would come with all kinds of expectations on her part. He only had sex with uncomplicated women who knew better than to expect more from him. He'd learned long ago not to want or expect more either.

Sex?

He did not want to sleep with Faith—which was the truth. Sleep had nothing to do with what he'd found himself thinking of last night, this morning when he'd awakened.

He didn't like being aware of her. Of waking with the scent of her perfume and sound of her laughter fresh in his mind.

"I'm allowed to take a non-working lunch break." Shoving her glasses up the straight slant of her pert little nose, she looked as exasperated as she sounded.

"You should have told me. I'd planned to review the information we compiled last night prior to making a final decision on the initial patients to receive the procedure." Why was she being so evasive? Who was she having lunch with? The mystery man? Perhaps they weren't having lunch at all? "Cancel your plans."

Annoyance flashed in her eyes, surprising him. Faith never argued with him, never went against his wishes, never made lunch plans. She ate lunch with *him*. The only time they didn't share a working lunch was if *he* made other plans.

Glancing at her watch with a disgusted look, her shoulders fell a notch, slamming him with unaccustomed guilt rather than the satisfaction that should have come with knowing he was about to get his way. And what was with her and looking at her watch the past two days? Faith wasn't a clock-watcher.

"Fine." She exhaled deeply, "I was fooling myself that I had time to get my hair done and find a dress for the wedding in an hour anyway."

Vale stopped walking, standing perfectly still

on the sidewalk as throngs of people continued to bustle around them without missing a beat. He stared at Faith, and decided that, yes, like he was often told, he really was a selfish jerk. Here Faith was going to his cousin's wedding, spending the weekend working and protecting him from his family's matchmaking, and he hadn't given one thought to the fact that she might want to have her hair done or buy a new outfit. He hadn't given one thought that Faith was a woman with normal female urges, like desiring new outfits for social events.

Then again, during the entire time he'd known Faith, she hadn't acted like other women. Why should he have thought this weekend would be any different? If he'd thought about what she'd wear, he would have said scrubs or maybe a hyper-masculine gray suit and a hairstyle any librarian would be proud of.

"What time is your appointment?"

She didn't glance up. "It doesn't matter. I'll cancel."

But beneath the clear lenses of her glasses, her eyes had grown shiny and his sense of guilt gnawed at his belly, threatening to give him an ulcer if he didn't make amends. What was the aura about her that made him want to make her happy?

"Why did you leave your appointment until so late? Surely you could have shopped for a dress earlier in the week?"

Her mouth dropped and if glares were bullets he'd be six feet under. "Did you really just ask me that when you've had me at the office every night this week until after ten?" Realizing what she'd said, her jaw dropped even lower. "Not that I mind," she recanted. "I like my job. It's just… well…" She fumbled, taking a deep breath. "I don't have anything appropriate to wear to the wedding and I've been thinking about getting my hair cut anyway. I thought prior to the wedding would be as good a time as any."

His gaze immediately went to her hair. She always kept her hair pulled tightly into the professional bun. He couldn't recall ever having seen her hair down. Odd, considering how long they'd known each other.

What did she look like with her hair down?

He was struck with the need to know, the need to see her dark blond locks loose. Would the strands barely brush her shoulders or would they cascade down her back?

"Get your hair done." He ran his gaze over the sleeked-back strands nestled at her nape. "But not short, okay?"

He wasn't sure why he added the last. The length of her hair was none of his business. If she wanted to go bald, other than their patients' reactions, he had no right to say a word.

"I probably wouldn't have had time anyway, Vale. Thinking I did was wishful thinking."

He'd give her time. He owed her that much. She was saving him from his family's match-making.

"I'll see your patients."

Her face flushing, she shook her head, eyeing him as if he must be running a fever. "That won't be necessary."

But it was necessary.

"Look, Faith, I'm a slave driver. There's no question of that." He raked his fingers through his hair, wondering why the spring air that had felt so good moment's earlier now cut into him. "But you're right. Your lunches are your own, even if I do monopolize them. Go. Get your hair done however you want. Buy yourself a new dress."

"But—"

"Actually," he withdrew his wallet from his back pocket. "Take the rest of the afternoon off and buy yourself a dress for tonight, too. On me."

Her face pale, she stared at the cash in his hand. "I can't take your money."

"Sure you can," he teased. "You do every pay period."

"That's different." Her lips pursed. "I've earned my paycheck. This is different."

"Look, it's my fault you need new clothes and to have your hair done. It's only fair I pay." He shoved the cash into her palm, closed her hand around the money. How his fingers lingered, how he wanted to hold her hand for real, surprised him. He forced his smile to stay in place despite his unhappiness with his wayward fingers, despite his confusion over what the hell was going on with his reactions to Faith.

"Go," he ordered. "Have fun, and I'll pick you up from your place."

"Yep, Yoda," Faith agreed with the yapping dog bouncing around at her feet while she studied her new image in the mirror, "I barely recognize myself, too."

She couldn't believe the difference a decent hair cut, highlighting, and facial could make. A fairy godmother waving a magic wand and singing "Bippity-boppity-boo" couldn't have conjured a more drastic transformation.

Faith hadn't had time over the past few years to worry about her appearance. Instead she'd focused on studying for boards and becoming the best neurologist she could be. Then she'd landed a dream job with Wakefield and Fishe straight out of school, an opportunity of a lifetime she wouldn't screw up.

So, no, her appearance hadn't been a priority in eons, if ever, but, wow, an afternoon of pampering could sure make a huge difference in the way a girl looked and felt about herself.

Or maybe it was the contacts burning her eyes that only made her think she was seeing such a difference.

She'd worn disposable lenses during high school and as an undergraduate, but during medical school she'd gone almost exclusively to her glasses. She'd bought the contacts at her check-up a couple of weeks ago during lunch when Vale had been in a meeting with Marcus. But she hadn't taken time to even pull them out of her handbag. When the make-up artist at the salon had complained about Faith's glasses, she'd surprised him by producing the sealed vials containing the lenses.

Then there were the clothes.

Clothes as in plural.

She hadn't wanted to spend Vale's money, had felt guilty taking the cash. She could have found a way to slip the money back to him over the weekend. Perhaps she still would as she still wasn't comfortable with the thought of him paying for her shopping trip even if, in a way, he was right. It was his fault she'd needed a new dress. She certainly wouldn't have gone shopping if he hadn't pressed her into accompanying him.

She hadn't just bought a new dress. She'd bought three. And new underwear that made her feel delectably feminine and a bit of a siren at heart. Really, would she like the black thigh highs and garter belt quite so much otherwise?

Then there was the daring bikini she'd let the sales clerk talk her into, even though she'd never have the nerve to wear the deep red triangles in public.

She'd also bought a few semi-casual outfits. She wasn't really sure what Saturday's schedule would require, but she felt prepared for whatever came up. Of course, she'd had to drag out the largest of her suitcases to fit in all her purchases, but that was a small price to pay for being prepared.

Then again, maybe she'd gone overboard and Vale would read her make-over as a desperate plea for him to notice her as he had the night before.

Was her make-over a desperate plea for him to notice her?

She winced. No, if he hadn't noticed her for the woman she was on the inside, she certainly didn't want him to notice her for changes to her outer appearance. Not that the changes were that glamorous, anyway. Not in comparison to the supermodels usually draped across Vale's arms. Regardless, Vale wasn't interested in investing time with a woman. He got what he wanted and moved on. Next.

What he wanted from her was a working weekend where she played decoy to his mother's matchmaking.

Still, she'd be lying if she said she wasn't eager to see his reaction when she opened her apartment door. Quite simply she didn't look like the same woman he'd walked to the salon. And had it been her imagination or had he touched her hand a half dozen times spreading wildfires up her arm?

She bent and picked up Yoda. "Hey, boy, are you going to miss me? Hmm, are you?" She rubbed her nose to the dog's, laughing when he licked her. "Now quit that before you mess up my make-up." At the dog's head quirk, she laughed again. "I know, I know, I've never cared before, but tonight's special and I suspect this make-up isn't doggy-kisses proof."

Yoda licked her again, obviously not caring if her make-up was doggy-kiss proof or not. Scratching the miniature poodle behind his ears, she praised him, telling him how much she was going to miss him over and over, and reminding him how much he loved visiting Mrs. Beasley.

"Come on. I guess I should go drop you there before His Highness arrives." Cradling the dog in one arm, she gathered the diaper bag of dog goodies she'd packed him. "Let's get you next door."

Saying goodbye was difficult, but once inside Mrs. Beasley's, Yoda didn't seem to mind at all that Faith would be gone all weekend.

"No worries. He's Miss Cupcake's favorite guest," the older woman promised as they walked to the door. "She and I will take good care of Yoda, and you know I can use the extra money from dog-sitting."

Standing in the doorway, Faith leaned in and kissed Mrs. Beasley's weathered cheek. "I know. Bye, love you."

Closing the door, she turned to go back to her apartment and caught Vale in the hallway admiring her backside.

Vale blinked, attempting to clear his eyes.

That stunning derrière and killer legs he'd been admiring were Faith's?

He'd known she had a decent body, he wasn't blind, but her scrubs did nothing to accent her curves and apparently everything to hide them. Where had all that tantalizing flesh come from?

And her eyes.

He'd always liked Faith's eyes. But without her glasses they were huge, luminous, *tempting*.

No, he wasn't tempted by Faith.

Only he was.

Tempted to push her up against the apartment hallway wall, push up that nipped-at-the-waist tease of a skirt, and thrust between those long, long legs.

Where had she gotten those legs and why hadn't he noticed before?

Okay, so he had noticed a time or two when she'd had on one of those ugly gray suits she sometimes wore that she had great calves. The kind that plumped out when she reached for a book on a high shelf. But Lord help him at the expanse of thigh on display beneath the hem of the dress she wore now.

And her shoulders.

His fingers itched to rub over her bare skin. He'd never seen her shoulders bare before. There should be laws against covering shoulders like hers. He liked what he saw beneath the stringy dress straps. He liked it a lot. Her hair was up but, unlike her work style, long, highlighted tendrils hung low, daring him to set free the caught-up strands. The style revealed the tantalizing curve of her exposed neck. He wanted to kiss her there, taste her, work his way down, sensitize every neuron in her body.

Oh, hell. He was in trouble. He couldn't bring her to his parents' house like this, with him on the verge of busting through his pants just from looking at her, with him practically licking his lips in anticipation of her feminine delights.

"My money bought that?"

Her lower lip disappeared between her teeth. Uncertainty marred her expression. She glanced down at the blue dress she wore, exposing those long legs that had his brain working overtime—or, more like, not working at all.

"You don't like my dress?"

"What's not to like? You're gorgeous, Faith." The insecurity in her eyes had him scampering to put the glow back on her face. "Absolutely stunning."

Her gaze lifted to his and a smile played at her lips. "Really?"

He laughed at her obvious fishing for a compliment.

"Best return I've ever gotten off a few hundred bucks." Immediately, he could see he'd said the wrong thing. Again. And again the overwhelming need to repair the damage filled him. "Why do you hide yourself away when you were obviously meant to be admired by the world?"

But this time she didn't light back up, just moved past him and unlocked her apartment door.

Knowing he'd unintentionally hurt her, but not sure how, he followed her into the apartment and grabbed her wrist, turning her to face him.

"I didn't mean that the way you obviously took it. You're a beautiful woman, Faith, always. If what I said made you think I was implying otherwise, then you're wrong. Nothing could be further from the truth."

Without looking his way, she shrugged. "Okay."

Placing his finger beneath her chin, he forced her to look at him and felt his heart kick up at the swirling emotion in her green-apple-candy eyes. Had he ever seen bigger, more expressive eyes? "No, it's not okay. I've hurt you."

"I'm not some fragile ninny who needs coddling, Vale." Her gaze lowered, settling near his throat. "We're business colleagues going away for a working weekend at your cousin's wedding. There's no reason for you to explain your comment. I know I made a big change."

Like a beautiful butterfly emerging from its cocoon. The same on the inside, yet so utterly different on the outside.

He felt humbled to have played a role in the transformation, even such a tiny role. Yet he wanted her to see what he saw—a stunning young woman.

His thumb stroked along her jaw line, caressing the soft skin, noting the pink flush spreading across her cheeks, the parting of her pouty pink lips, the way his heart beat faster in his chest when her stunned gaze met his.

Vale did something totally out of character.

He lowered his lips to hers.

Faith's knees wobbled. Firecrackers detonated in her chest, pounding her heart against her ribcage, demanding freedom to burst into a million projectile pieces.

No way was Vale kissing her!

If a trip to the salon and an upscale dress boutique was all it had taken to get his lips on hers, why hadn't she gone shopping months ago?

Had her hair streaked with strands of gold and a trained professional paint her face?

What was she thinking? This was Vale. Her boss. She should not be letting him kiss her.

He cupped her cheeks, drawing her closer, tasting her lips with a softness that belied the tough man she knew him to be.

She stood stock still, hands at her side, sure if she moved or even breathed, the fantasy would disappear, a pleasurable vapor she'd grasped at but failed to hold on to.

For eighteen months she'd wondered what this man tasted like, what his lips would feel like against hers, and now he was kissing her. So she gave in to the desire erupting within her, kissed him back, tasted his lips, opened her mouth to let him inside and hoped he'd never let her go, that he'd never stop kissing her.

Tiny explosions ripped through her one after another in the wake of his tongue thrusting into her mouth.

He was no longer cupping her face but her bottom, pulling her fully against his hard body.

He was hard. Amazingly, eye-wideningly…
Oh, my!

As much as Faith wanted to spread her arms wide and welcome him, to take whatever he would offer her, she had to stop him before she completely lost her mind and became one of the many women to move in and out of his life.

Before he realized just how much she wanted him. Because Vale only wanted one thing from women. She had to think of her career.

She pushed against his chest. "Stop."

He lifted his head, his lids half covering his desire-laden eyes. He wanted her. He had kissed her, wanted her, might have carried her to her sofa and made heart-pounding, thigh-slapping love to her if she hadn't told him to stop.

Her head spun. Her eyes blurred. Her equilibrium shifted.

Regret that she'd stopped him filled her, making her wish she'd dragged him into her bedroom rather than push him away. But makeover or not, she wasn't one of his playthings. She was his employee, a physician with plans to have a phenomenal career within his neuro clinic, and not by sleeping her way to the top.

Although with her lack of experience, sleeping with Vale might get her sacked instead of promoted.

"Why did you do that?" Wiping the back of her hand across her mouth, she stepped back, wishing she wasn't shaking, wishing she didn't want to beg him to kiss her again. She had to take control of the situation prior to him figuring out just how much she wanted to jump back into his arms.

"You needed to be kissed."

If he thought his hot kisses had left her any less in need of being kissed, he was wrong.

All he'd managed to do was to show her what she'd been missing, what she now knew she desperately wanted. His kisses.

Determined to salvage her pride, she frowned, wishing he wasn't still touching her. "Says who?"

He rubbed his thumb across her lower lip. "Says me."

A shiver whipped through her body, prickling

her flesh. "Even if I did need to be kissed, that's not your place. I told you on the day I agreed to this trip with you—I won't be lumped into the category of one of your girls."

He seemed to consider her comment a moment. "You're wrong, Faith. Kissing you is exactly my place. This weekend, you are my girl."

CHAPTER THREE

OF ALL the arrogant comments Faith had ever heard!

She was not Vale's girl. Just because she'd agreed to a working weekend to save him from his family's matchmaking, that did not make her his property and certainly not one of the arm decorations he paraded around New York's social scene.

She snuck a glance at his powerful profile. Staring straight ahead, watching traffic as he drove to Cape May, he looked exactly the same as he always had. Same sun-kissed light brown hair, same sparkling blue eyes that could pierce a person's soul with their intensity, same handsome face. Same calm presence, completely untouched by the kiss they'd shared.

He was whistling, for goodness' sake. An

upbeat melody that was slowly driving her insane.

Urgh. He frustrated her. Infuriated her. He'd kissed her. Taken notice of the fact that she was of the opposite sex and kissed her. A toe-curling, thigh-melting, neuron synapse-searing, honest-to-goodness kiss.

Yes, she'd been the one to stop him, because she'd had to. But she'd wanted him to take her into his arms, tell her he'd been a fool not to see what was right beneath his nose, and could she ever forgive him?

Okay, so that was pure fantasy and not the kind of thing that happened in reality. But men like Vale kissing her didn't happen in her reality either.

At least, nothing like that had ever happened before.

"You're staring a hole through my head."

How did he know that when he hadn't glanced away from the traffic on the New Jersey Parkway?

"Impossible."

As if she hadn't just taken a shot at him, he grinned. "I meant figuratively, not literally."

"I knew that," she pointed out, determined not to let him get the upper hand. "I was referring to your hard-headedness making staring a hole through your head impossible in any shape, form, or fashion. Figuratively or literally."

He laughed, a husky male sound that warmed her insides. "Point taken."

Eyes narrowed, she twisted in her seat to more easily look at him. "Are you mocking me?"

She'd swear his lips twitched with amusement. What was so funny? He'd kissed her and turned her world upside down and now he was laughing at her? If he hadn't been driving, she'd… she'd…well, she'd have come up with some horrendous punishment, if her life wasn't literally in his hands.

"Relax, Faith." He glanced away from the road long enough to meet her gaze. "Maybe we shouldn't have brought the patient profiles with us."

"Why not?"

"This isn't going to be a working weekend after all."

She wouldn't gulp. Not even if she really, really needed to gulp.

"Why?" She gulped.

"Because I've been working you too hard, and you need to relax, have a little fun."

"I have fun." She didn't want him thinking she was a dull Jane. Even if she was a dull Jane who worked most of the time and spent too much of her precious little spare time working even more so as to impress him when next they met.

"With whomever you were kissing goodbye in apartment 907?"

Mrs. Beasley? She started to laugh, but then realized he was serious, had made note of her neighbor's apartment number, and, most surprising, sounded a tad bit jealous.

Was it possible? Could a make-over and one kiss have him feeling possessive? Oh, what was she thinking? He was probably just worried that if she had a life she wouldn't be at his beck and call for work. Just look at how he'd reacted to her making lunch plans that didn't involve work.

"Apartment 907 is my neighbor."

"And you tell this neighbor you love him?"

He'd heard that? And why was he using his annoyed voice on her? She glared at him in silence. Even with only being able to see his profile, she could see his expression harden.

"It's a simple question, Faith. No harm in answering."

Oh, enough was enough.

"My neighbor is a seventy-year-old sweetheart who dog-sits for me while I'm at work. I was dropping off Yoda, not telling a man I loved him. Not that it's any of your business if I was."

His brow rose. "Yoda?"

"My dog."

"You have a dog?"

"Yes, a miniature poodle."

"A miniature poodle?" His nose curled with unpleasantness. "Not much in the way of protection."

"You'd be surprised. Yoda might be small but he has the heart of a lion."

He smirked. "You're not one of those women

who puts clothes and bows and such on her pet, are you?"

Faith didn't answer.

He burst out laughing. "You are, aren't you? My little miss organized neurologist plays dress-up with her dog."

She took a deep breath. "Yoda happens to like his Darth Poodle pajamas."

Vale snorted. "May the force be with him, because he's going to need all the help he can get when the other dogs who still have theirs get through with him."

"Yeah, well, other than Miss Cupcakes, Mrs. Beasley's female Chihuahua, Yoda doesn't spend a lot of time around other dogs. He'd like to, but I'm always at work and Mrs. Beasley's idea of a walk is to the end of the block and back for potty breaks."

He glanced toward her. "I'm sensing some latent resentment. Are you telling me you're working too many hours?"

"I am working too many hours." What was wrong with her? Why was she telling him this? Eighteen months she'd busted her butt without a single word of complaint. Eighteen months she'd gone above and beyond whatever needed to be done just to impress him.

What had they highlighted her hair with? Truth serum?

Or was his kiss what had loosened her tongue?

"Which is why we should forget the Parkinson project for the weekend and just enjoy ourselves. The rest will be good for both of us, will have our minds refreshed when we return on Sunday," he mused, not looking at her. "Too bad we didn't bring Yoda with us. He might have gotten a chance to show off his fancy duds on the beach."

Faith's gaze narrowed in his direction, not that he noticed as he was watching traffic and not her. "Quit making fun of my dog."

"If you put clothes on your dog, you have to expect him to be made fun of. By real men and real dogs."

"I expect no such thing and Yoda is a real dog. The best dog. The sweaters are to keep him warm."

"And here I thought that's what fur was for."

He shot a horrified look her way. "You didn't shave him, did you?"

"No." Taking an exasperated breath, she shook her head, pursed her lips at him. "I know what you're doing, and it isn't going to work."

He had the audacity to glance at her, all innocence and good looks. "What isn't going to work?"

As if he didn't know exactly what he was doing.

"What you're doing."

"Which is?"

"Trying to get me flustered about the dog so that I will forget to make my case regarding this not being a working weekend." She fixed him with a determined glare. "This is a working weekend, Vale."

Changing lanes on the parkway, he passed a slower car. "What's wrong with us just having some fun?"

Was he kidding? "The only reason I'm here is because this is a working weekend."

"That's not true. I asked you to accompany

me this weekend because my mother was determined to parade every single female at the wedding in front of me in the hope I'll not be able to resist making a walk down a long aisle to a short-noosed rope." He pulled off the parkway, zipped through the EZ Pass lane at the toll booth, and headed toward downtown Cape May. "With you by my side, she'll leave me alone. I can spend time with my family without having to call out the National Guard."

The National Guard? Did he expect such a rush of female would-be suitors? Casting another quick look at him, she decided that, yes, he probably did and rightly so. Forget his money, power and prestige, Dr. Vale Wakefield was still the finest catch in New York.

For the weekend she was to defend his bachelorhood? Where was the 1-800 hotline to the National Guard? She'd be the one needing reinforcements.

"She won't buy that I'm anything more than a colleague."

Vale shot her a quick look. "Why wouldn't she?"

Should she list the reasons? Write him a thesis perhaps? "I'm not your type."

"Obviously, you are." And obviously he found her comment amusing since he chuckled.

"What's that supposed to mean? You like tall, willowy women with IQs lower than their bust sizes," she reminded him.

"I kissed you," he parried.

As if those three little words explained everything.

She bit her lower lip. "Why did you?"

"I wanted to."

He'd wanted to. Pleasure bubbled inside her like just uncorked champagne, overflowing with rich, foamy giddiness, intoxicating her senses.

She was drugged. Drugged by the insanity being around a man as potent as Vale caused. She didn't want this, didn't want to feel this way. Not about him or any man.

"What about what I wanted?"

"Are you saying you didn't want me to kiss you? Because I don't believe you." His expression said, Yeah, right. Tell me another one.

"I stopped you," she reminded him, chin high.

"Not until after a good bit of tongue thrusting and spit swapping had taken place. Face it, Faith, you wanted me to kiss you as much as I wanted to kiss you."

"Eww." Ignoring his second sentence, she wrinkled her nose at his coarse words. "Don't be gross, Vale."

"I was making a point."

"Grossing me out is more like it."

They came to a stop at a traffic light and he turned to face her, his eyes boring into her soul. "Kissing me grossed you out?"

With his gaze fixed on her, she couldn't lie to him. Not even when that was what she really wanted to do. Instead she blurted out the embarrassing facts in the most revealing of ways.

"Kissing you didn't gross me out." Except at the abandoned way she'd kissed him back when she knew better.

"What did kissing me do?" His voice was husky, confident, as if he knew exactly what his kisses did to women.

Of course he knew what his kisses did to women.

Just as she knew.

Kissing Vale made women crazy, fanatical, addicted. She knew that. She'd watched his effect on women, knew the dangers of being near him in any capacity not business-related.

Vale didn't mix business and pleasure. He just didn't. Not ever.

Only he had by kissing her.

"Kissing you made me think I'm crazy for agreeing to this when I had the opportunity to spend a weekend relaxing at home because you'd have been otherwise occupied, not calling me to meet you at the office for yet more work."

His eyes narrowed into deep blue slits. "You don't like working with me?"

"I love my job, but someday I do hope to have a life outside work."

"What kind of life?"

Why on earth had she started this conversation? Or had he started it? Either way, she wanted out.

"The usual," she said dryly, grateful they'd moved beyond what his kisses did to her, but hoping he'd let their new subject drop.

"What usual?"

Of course he wouldn't. Not the great Dr. Vale Wakefield, New York's most eligible bachelor.

"You know," she admitted reluctantly. "A house in some smarmy little suburb that I can call my own. A yard for Yoda to dig holes in. A neighborhood where I can take him for long walks."

His brows drew together in a deep furrow, his lips tight with displeasure. "That's your idea of the usual? What about marriage? Children? That usual?"

Maybe that was usual for some women. To Faith there was nothing usual about marriage or having children. Not in the marriages she'd witnessed. And, although she was mightily attracted to Vale, she didn't kid herself that it was anything more than that. Men didn't stick around. Even men who promised to, and Vale wasn't the type to make such promises to begin with.

"Women who want to make it in a high-powered career shouldn't reveal to the boss that they also want to have a family," she answered in the hope of steering him in a direction other than the truth. "Not if they want to be taken seriously."

"You think I'd penalize you if you said you wanted a family?"

"I think you're more likely to advance someone who didn't have to take time off for maternity leave and pediatric visits." Dear Lord, someone really had slipped her some truth serum. She couldn't shut up. "My career is important to me. I told you that from the beginning."

"Yes, you were quite vocal that day."

Why did the way he spoke make her think he was mocking her?

"Laugh if you want to, but I'm serious." She shrugged. "After I've achieved my career goals I'll think about marriage."

Not that she'd want marriage ever. She was more than happy with Yoda. Her dog would never leave her for another woman—except perhaps Mrs. Beasley and her cutie pie Miss Cupcake.

He seemed to digest her comment. "After you've achieved your career goals you plan to marry and have kids?"

"After I achieve my career goals…" tired of the picking apart of her life goals, she gestured toward the green light that had changed at some point during their conversation, but neither had noticed "…I'll make plans for the rest of my life."

Faith had already decided she wasn't going to allow herself to be intimidated by the Wakefield family fortune. She just wasn't.

Yes, she knew the family was as iconic as the Vanderbilts, the Kennedys, and the Fords, but Wakefields were human beings, too, just like her. No better. No worse.

Telling herself this and actually being able to keep her jaw from dropping when Vale whipped his low-slung red road devourer into the circle drive of a house that looked more like a hotel were two different things. Holy medulla oblongata! This was really just a house?

"This is your family's beach home?"

He glanced at the lumbering three-story beige house with balconies jutting out on every level. "The East Coast one, yes. My mother had the old house torn down, and this one built a few years ago. Personally, I preferred the former one."

They had a beach house for each coast? Had torn down their previous beach house to rebuild another? Somehow, she doubted the East Coast home had been torn down due to being rundown. Faith let that digest. Sure, Vale had money, lots of money, but the side she generally saw of him could have been just another hard-working physician, not the son of a family worth billions.

Except for the society-page photos with women hanging all over him. Those she could do without.

Vale switched off the ignition, but made no move to get out of the car. Stretching forward, his arms wrapped around the steering-wheel, he took a deep breath. "Remind me why I'm doing this wedding again."

Wondering exactly the same thing, Faith tore her gaze away from the monstrosity where they'd be staying and unbuckled her seat belt with shaky fingers. "Because your cousin Sharon expects you to be here."

"And Sharon must get her way."

Did she? Faith had never met any of Vale's family, but could only imagine that they must be used to the world bowing at their privileged Italian leather–covered feet. Just looking at the enormous house before her made her knees want to buckle. She was so out of her league.

"Must run in the family," she mused.

"Must." He grinned, opening the door of his car that probably cost more than triple her annual salary. "Let's go in. I'll grab our luggage later."

First checking her appearance to make sure she wasn't committing some faux pas such as lipstick on her teeth, Faith reached for her door-handle and was surprised when the door opened before she could.

"What are you doing?" She blinked up at Vale. Lord, the man was fast. In so many ways, a total speed demon.

"Opening your door."

"Why?"

"I already told you why," he said with exaggerated patience. "This weekend, you're my girl. A gentleman opens the door for his girl."

A thousand birds took flight in her belly at once.

"No, Vale." She spoke just as slowly as he had so there would be no misunderstanding between them. "For the record, I'm not your girl and you are not a gentleman."

Reaching for her hand to help her out, he gave her a mock sympathetic look. "You're wasting your breath. We've already established that we Wakefields always get our way."

True, but being here as his colleague for a working weekend was one thing, pretending to be his girl or whatever it was he wanted from her was something completely different. Not when part of her wanted to be his girl. For real.

"And to set the record straight—" his grin was lethal "—I'm always a gentleman when it comes to the ladies."

Stepping from the low-slung sports car, she turned to face him, determined to make him understand. "Vale, I won't—"

Tugging on her hand, he pulled her flush to him and she forgot how to breathe. The respiratory centers of her brain literally shut down and left her woozy.

"Sure you will, and you'll have fun. I promise."

Looking into his twinkling eyes, Faith believed him. Being his girl, even for a weekend, would be fun. Only then she'd have to pay the piper the price for that fun. And, dear Lord, could she please have some oxygen in her lungs please?

"Don't look now, but we're being watched."

She started turning toward the house, but Vale's forehead lowered to rest against hers, and, grinning, he said, "My mother and aunt are standing at the window and I told you not to look."

"Yes, but if this isn't a working weekend, you're not my boss, are you?" she bit out, trying not to gasp for air.

He started to speak, but she rushed on.

"I'm not doing anything I don't want to do and you can't make me because I don't have to do as you say. Not away from work. And when I don't do as Your Highness commands, you're not going to say a word to this lady who has her own mind and isn't afraid to use it." She pulled away from him, shut her car door herself, then smiled as pretty as you please, only feeling slightly dizzy in the process, especially when he immediately recaptured her in his arms. "Because you're a gentlemen when it comes to the ladies, remember?"

CHAPTER FOUR

VALE conceded that Faith had made a great point, wondering why he was suddenly as nervous as he'd been during his first stint in the operating room, wondering why he cared so much what Faith thought of his family, why it felt so right to have her in his arms when nothing could be further than the truth.

His gaze lowered to her all-too-kissable lips. "I'm always the boss, Faith. Always."

Eyes wide, she swallowed. "Your family is originally from Philadelphia, aren't they?"

So she wanted to change the subject? He'd let her, but he wasn't letting her go, even if she was squirming against him, trying to free herself. Actually, he should let her go because she was squirming against him and he was rapidly getting turned on. Talking about his family should cure that.

"Yes, Philadelphia is their home base, but we spend more time together here." With his arms still wrapped around her waist, he glanced toward the house his mother had thought they'd needed a few years back. He missed the more traditional beach house she'd had torn down to make room for its too-modern, too-big replacement. She hadn't been able to bear the original beach house after his father had died, though, and Vale had never contradicted her claims that they'd needed more room.

"These days," he continued, "it's rare for the entire family to be together, though. Holidays and special occasions. That's about it."

"You worked through last Christmas," she reminded him, no longer struggling to free herself and staring at him with her amazing eyes. He'd swear he could look into her eyes for hours on end without getting bored. Not with the ever-changing gold flecks and the deep rings around her green irises.

"I flew to Philly for Christmas morning and spent the day with my family." He pressed his palms into her low back, relishing how she molded to him, how his gut tightened with the desire to feel her naked beneath him.

"You were back home that night, working," she gulped, staring at him as if she could read his mind and wasn't sure what to think of this change in him. Hell, he didn't know what to think of these new reactions to her either.

"How do you know I came back that night?"

She rolled her eyes. "Because, no thought whatsoever to my holiday, you called, wanting me to assist on the Parkinson's article you were writing."

Ah, now he remembered. He'd been alone, digging through medical records, compiling data for his article, wishing Faith was there. Before he'd thought twice about the day being Christmas, he'd dialed her cell number. "You came."

"Yes," she agreed, her eyes taking on a faraway look. "You called, and I came running. Even on Christmas Day. My career is important to me, remember? Having my name next to yours in a prestigious medical journal looks good on my résumé."

Had she been with her someone special? Unwrapping presents and sitting on the sofa, watching multicolored lights flicker on the tree?

"Did I interrupt a Christmas dinner?"

Her face pinched. "Nothing that I minded having interrupted."

"You weren't with lover-boy?"

"Who?"

"Whoever you spend your time with when you're not with me?"

"I spent Christmas Day with my mother and stepfather. Your call was a mixed blessing."

He'd met Faith's mother once. A vivacious woman with lots of spirit who'd stopped by the clinic unexpectedly. He'd liked her instantly, but a flustered Faith had rushed her mother and her stepfather out the door within minutes of their arrival. "What's your stepfather's name? Curtis?"

Nose curling, Faith sighed. "Curtis was her previous husband. This one's name is John."

"That's right. She remarried earlier this year. John Debellis, the stockbroker you don't like."

"It's not that I don't like him. John's okay." Her

lips thinned to white lines and her eyes stayed on her freshly manicured hands.

He'd never seen her nails painted, missed their usual natural gleam.

"I can tell you're jumping for joy over how okay he is."

"He's my stepfather. One of many I've had." She shrugged. "There's no point in liking him. Within another year or two he'll have found someone new and my mother will become involved with someone else that she'll likely go on to marry, and he'll do the same. It's the way life is."

Just how many times had Faith's mother been married?

He would have asked, but the front door flung open and his cousin bounded down the steps, flinging herself at him full force, practically knocking Faith out of his arms.

"Vale!"

Faith squared her shoulders, stood her ground, as if bracing herself for an unpleasant experience. Immediately that unwanted protectiveness came forth in Vale. Did she think his family wouldn't accept her?

"Meet my cousin Sharon." He set his cousin on the ground next to him, placed his hand low on Faith's back. "Don't mind her antics. She's been throwing herself at men since she was three."

Sharon slapped his arm. "Behave. You'll give your friend the impression I'm wild."

"You are wild," he replied, smiling indulgently at the blonde beauty he'd spent most of his youth exploring with, despite being two years older than her. In addition to their Wakefield blue eye color, they'd shared an adventurous spirit.

"Not any more." She flashed her ring finger in front of his face. A large, multi-faceted diamond twinkled in the sunshine.

"If Steve thinks a rock is going to make you settle down, he's in for it."

She grinned. "What makes you think Steve wants me to settle down?"

Vale threw his head back and laughed. "Brave man."

"Smart, scrumptious man." Sharon turned to

Faith and hugged her as enthusiastically as she'd leapt into Vale's arms.

He should have known his cousin would make Faith feel welcome. Sharon might be renowned for her outer beauty, but her real beauty came from within.

"It's so good to meet the woman Vale deems worthy of attending my wedding as his date." Sharon plopped a kiss on Faith's pale cheek. "You must be special."

"I'm more of a friend than date," she immediately corrected, her posture so perfect the sternest school matron would have applauded.

He stepped forward. "What Faith is trying to say is that we're co-workers and she doesn't want anyone to think she's trying to sleep her way to the top. Particularly me."

Red splotched her cheeks. Her gaze snapped to his and she outright glared.

Sharon burst out laughing, pulling a stiff Faith into another hug. "Oh, I like her, Vale. She's not a doormat like most of the women you hang out with. Keep her around, okay?"

Grinning, Vale followed the two women into the house.

He had every intention of keeping Faith around.

Vale's mother looked more like an older sister than a woman of more than fifty years. Actually, she looked like grown-up Barbie come to life, buzzing in and out of the main living area of the biggest house Faith had ever set foot in.

The Wakefields' beach home. Their second home. Or would it be their third home as they had a west coast home, too? Hadn't she read something about an estate on the coast of Italy, too? The whole idea of having multiple homes of this magnitude made Faith's head spin.

She'd never had a single-unit home, had always lived in an apartment building or college dorm, had always lived in New York. How boring Vale must find her compared to the well-traveled women he usually spent his non-working time with.

But she wasn't going to let him push her around, or push her into a physical relationship just because she was convenient. Not when her career was at stake. Otherwise she'd be leaping into his arms with just as much exuberance as his cousin had—only Faith's motives would have been much less pure.

His mother had rushed them inside, thrust drinks into their hands, and directed them to the living room that was double the size of Faith's entire apartment. Long rectangular windows along every wall boasted panoramic views of the sun going down over the Atlantic. Absolutely breathtaking. Absolutely terrifying. She was so out of her league.

"We're so glad Vale brought you this weekend, Faith." His mother leaned in to give her a quick air kiss. Diamonds the size of Texas sparkled on Virginia Wakefield's manicured fingers. "Be sure to let me know if you need another drink. Or if you forgot anything from home. I always keep extra bare essentials."

Guilt swam through her at the warm reception Vale's family greeted her with since she was there under what she considered false pretenses. She'd been so leery of their wealth and figured her lack thereof would be an insurmountable barrier, but they'd been nothing but kind to her from the moment Vale's exuberant cousin had jumped him.

"I had your luggage put in your room. Faith's, too."

"Yes, Mom," Vale intoned as his mother flitted toward Sharon's younger sister, Angela.

Faith turned to him. Her luggage was in his room? She supposed that asking for a separate room would raise a few eyebrows. Obviously the women he brought home slept in his room. But she was not one of his women and had no intention of losing her brain this weekend.

Her heart, well, she planned to keep that closely guarded as well because falling for him would be way too easy when he already occupied so much of her thoughts.

Her suitcase was in his room.

She wanted to say something, but bit her tongue. She'd put him on the floor, because if he thought they were sleeping in the same bed, he had another think coming.

Since arriving, he'd been unusually quiet. Unusually attentive. Probably in an effort to convince his family they were truly involved so they wouldn't start up with the matchmaking.

"Seeing you with your family almost makes you seem like an ordinary man." Right, because ordinary men drank Cristal from real crystal while walking on gleaming marble floors with million-dollar paintings hanging on the walls. It was enough to make a girl's neuron synapses fuse.

"I don't want you to think I'm ordinary."

She almost snorted. As if.

"No one would ever think you're ordinary, Vale," she assured in a purposely condescending tone.

His lips twitched in amusement. "You have a sharp tongue, Faith Fogarty."

"That's why you hired me," she reminded him. "My sharp tongue and sharper wit."

Vale threw his head back and laughed. Reaching out, he took her hand into his and lifted it to his mouth. "You might just be right about that."

What was he doing?

Why wasn't she stopping him?

Why were her knees trembling?

Why was every cell in her body going berserk, wanting to get closer and closer to him?

"Come on. Let's head outdoors," Sharon called, rushing everyone out the elaborate glass French doors that led onto a patio boasting a sparkling blue pool and hot tub, along with privacy created by the sand dunes behind the back yard.

A large white marquee had been set up along the back side of the property where the wedding reception would take place. On the opposite side, white chairs had been lined up in neat rows facing a gazebo where the bride and groom would stand, their attendants on the sides.

Still reeling from Vale's attention, Faith sat in one of the chairs near the middle and watched as Sharon ordered everyone around like a five-star general.

Thirty minutes later, Faith watched Vale take his place yet again two spots down from the groom, watched as they ran through the events one last time. He was bored but humoring his family and as much as she wanted him to be enough of a distraction to fully occupy her mind, for once he wasn't.

Sitting was pure torture. Being there was pure torture in so many ways. Each time the wedding march started, bile sloshed in her stomach, burning her throat, making her clench and unclench her fingers.

She detested weddings.

Had from the very first one she'd attended.

That had been the moment she'd had to admit to herself that her father wouldn't be coming home ever again. That she'd never have her happy family back.

That her father had truly abandoned her and her mother.

That her mother had moved on and so should she. And although her mother moved on, time and again, Faith never had.

Next to Faith, Virginia clapped her hands and sighed, apparently not suffering from a similar distaste for weddings.

"Oh," she sighed. "Everything is just perfect."

Perfect, because that's what weddings were.

Gag. Gag. Gag. Faith resisted the urge to put

her finger in her mouth and stimulate her glos-
sophayngeal and vagus nerves. Instead, she
glanced back toward Vale.

He'd been looking at her, an odd expression on
his face. Not a bad expression, more a quizzical
one. Then he smiled, dimples digging into his
cheeks, tiny crinkles forming at the corners of
his brilliant eyes.

Faith no longer wanted to gag. Instead she
fought drooling. Vale Wakefield was one gorgeous man.

He winked and for the first time since they'd
come outside she felt a smile tugging at her lips.
How could he do that? Take her from misery to
better with a mere wink?

"He really likes you."

Reality kicked in as she turned to Vale's
mother and was once again slammed with guilt,
her stomach roiling at the tumultuous ups and
downs her emotions were taking. Deceiving this
gracious woman just felt wrong. "We work well
together."

"Of course, you do, dear." Virginia patted
her arm and smiled graciously. "You must or

he never would have invited you here. I'm so pleased that he did."

A man setting up the dance floor beneath the pulled-back sides of the tent caught Vale's mother's eyes and, with another quick pat and smile, she went off to direct the worker.

"Enjoying yourself?" Vale asked, coming up behind her, pulling her from the chair and wrapping his arms around her waist.

"Vale, don't," she bit out. Why was he being so touchy-feely? She wasn't sure how much more touchy-feely she could handle.

"Don't?" He didn't take the hint, didn't let her go. "I have to keep you close. You're here to protect me from my family."

"Sure," she snorted. "Because now that I've met them I see how scary they are."

"They scare you, too? Now you understand why I need you to intervene." His smile was contagious, and melted away the worry gnawing in her belly, melted her insides to silly feminine goop.

"They just want you to be happy." She stepped back, unable to deal with what being in his arms did to her. "If you don't want them matchmaking, just tell them."

"I'm so glad you suggested that, because I've never thought about just telling my mother that I'm not interested in meeting a nice girl and settling down."

She narrowed her gaze. "In case you're wondering, sarcasm does not become you."

"Haven't you heard? Everything becomes me." His movie-star white teeth flashed. Rather than saying anything, he took her hand and led her away from the wedding festivities and out toward the high gate that opened to the sand dunes behind the mansion. A private boardwalk led out to the billowing Atlantic.

Faith's breath caught at the beauty of the white-capped waves rolling in, at how the almost set sun painted the sky with pinks, purples, and blues.

For just a moment she wanted to believe this was real, that Vale had invited her to his parents' this weekend because he wanted to be with her, that he missed her as much as she missed him when they were apart. She wanted to believe that they were going for a walk on the beach, holding hands, sharing the moment when the sun dipped from the sky. Not for show, not as friends or colleagues, but as lovers.

And that when it was all over she wouldn't have a broken heart. She definitely wanted to believe that because otherwise how could she allow herself to even indulge in the fantasy?

"Why haven't you?" She slipped off her heels and wiggled her toes in the warm sand.

He glanced up from where he pulled off his shoes and socks, dropping them onto the sand, and rolled up the cuffs of his dark slacks. "Why haven't I what?"

He was so gorgeous. More breathtaking than the sunset. More beautiful. More what she wanted, but shouldn't.

She dropped her heels next to his shoes. "Met a nice girl and settled down."

"Don't start, Faith." He grabbed her hand and headed toward the surf.

"What?" She stumbled, trying to keep up with his pace as he dragged her behind him, sand flying up at her ankles.

"Matchmaking," he spat the word out. "I don't need you fixing me up with friends any more than I need my family doing so."

As if she'd fix Vale up with one of her friends. Besides, thanks to the long hours she worked, few of her friends would even claim her these days.

"I can assure you I'd never do that to any of my friends. I like them too much to introduce them to you."

"Good, because if I ever marry, I'll find the woman all by myself."

Which meant he hadn't already found her.

Not that Faith thought he had. Just that part of her had hoped someday he'd realize how good it might be between them. Then again, she imagined Vale was the kind of man who it was always good between.

Between the sheets, between the car seats, between the sand and the waves.

Where had that thought come from? She wasn't prone to lust. Was used to dealing with how he made her feel and usually did a great job of suppressing her baser instincts. So why hadn't she then?

She gulped, tearing her gaze from him to stare out at the ocean. Coming here with him had been a horrible mistake. One she'd likely live to regret.

"What about you?"

"Me?" She knew his gaze was on her, but she didn't dare look at him. He'd see too much in her eyes, would instantly realize that she'd met the man she wanted for all time during a job interview eighteen months ago.

No! She hadn't met the man she wanted for all time. Vale was not that man. There was no *that man*. All she felt for Vale was physical attraction and professional admiration. That was it. Nothing more.

"Why haven't you married?" he clarified, his words nipping at her soul as surely as the tide tugged at her feet.

"I imagine someday I'll meet someone who'll sweep me off my feet." Someone who'd make her forget how Vale's lips had felt against hers, how even now thoughts of him pushing her back onto the sand and kissing her danced through her mind. Not that she thought things would last with that man either. She didn't.

Men left. It was what they did best.

"And give you babies to take to soccer practice?"

She tried not to let images of blue-eyed imps dribbling the ball toward the goal take over her mind. She did not want to have Vale's babies. She didn't want babies period. Sure, the making them might be fun, but then she'd be like her mother, alone, raising a child.

Only her mother hadn't been able to stand being alone and had flitted from one loveless marriage to another, from one man who'd eventually leave her to another.

"I'm in no hurry at this point in my life to meet someone or even think about marriage and babies. My career is what's most important."

"Until you achieve your career goals?" he teased, but his eyes held a steely quality.

"It's not as if I'm going to reach a certain point, mark my career off my life to-do list, then move on to marriage and children, Vale." She glanced out at the horizon, spotting the silhouette of a ferry off in the distance. "Just that at some point down the line I'd like to believe I can have all the things I want."

She wouldn't remind him that what she wanted was a real house with a real yard for her dog to play in. No man required.

"You're a special woman, Faith. If anyone can ever have it all, I'm sure it's you."

She glanced at him, saw the sincerity on his face, and smiled. "Thank you, Vale. That quite simply might be the nicest thing you've ever said to me."

"You jest." His forehead wrinkled. "I've complimented you before."

"About my work, yes. Me? No."

He stopped walking, turned to face her. His hand squeezed hers reassuringly. "Just tonight I told you what a beautiful woman you are."

"Tthat's d-different," she stammered, wondering at the light in his eyes. Was it the reflection of the last golden rays dancing across the sky? Or was Vale looking at her as if she really was beautiful?

His brow lifted. "Because you don't believe me when I say that you are beautiful?"

"I've seen the women you date. I'm not even in the same league." Models, actresses, heiresses, he went through them all.

"True," he agreed, twisting the knife in her gut. He could at least have been polite and not said anything.

She'd never have him, knew she never would, and was foolish to have these momentary lapses where she dreamed she might.

"None of the women I've known hold a candle to you, Faith. Not a single one."

She wanted to look away, wanted to shield her eyes from his, but she couldn't. Not when he looked at her as if he believed what he said, as if he really did believe she was more beautiful than the women he escorted to New York's finest venues. What else had they put in her hair color other than truth serum? A dose of *hear what you want to hear*?

"Thank you," she said for lack of knowing what else to say but knowing the situation called for something. She was imagining the softening of his gaze, the pressure of his hand holding hers. "That's a kind thing to say."

"You don't make me feel kind, Faith."

She stared up at him. "No?"

"No." Had his mouth moved closer to hers?

She licked her lips, nervously, yet even as she did so, she'd instinctively known his gaze would follow her movements. She wasn't a fool, wasn't imagining this chemistry between them. Truth serum, gullibility, whatever, the sparks arcing between them would light up lower Manhattan. "What do I make you feel, Vale?"

Great question and one Vale wasn't sure of the answer to.

He wanted her. Which surprised him. Usually he was either instantly attracted to a woman or he wasn't attracted at all.

With all women, he got what he wanted with little effort. Faith was different. He'd spent more time with her than with any other woman, knew her better, had let her know him better, yet what did he really know? Not even the name of her mysterious boyfriend.

Vale immediately lowered his mouth to cover hers, telling himself the surge of emotion in his chest was not jealousy of a man he'd never met. Whatever, Faith's lips were sweet beneath his and pleasure soon replaced the unwanted emotional surge.

Soft, full, yielding, yet demanding, she returned his kiss. If there was another man in her life, their relationship couldn't be too serious. Otherwise Faith wouldn't kiss him back. Yet she didn't do so whole-heartedly, which gave him pause. He could read her every thought, feel the conflicting sensations swirling inside that brilliant mind of hers. She wanted him, yet she didn't.

He understood perfectly because he felt exactly the same.

"I want to make love to you, Faith, but I'm not willing to ruin our professional relationship."

Her eyes widened at his admission, greener than the most precious emerald.

"You're more important to me than a quick rumble between the sheets." His words said one thing, but he asked her a question with his eyes.

A question he knew the answer to, but asked all the same in the hope he was wrong about Faith.

"Professional relationship at stake or not, I'm not willing to be just a rumble between any man's sheets, Vale. I'm not you. I don't do casual sex."

He'd known, but still disappointment filled him at her response.

"Understood." He ran his fingers along her cheek, thinking her more beautiful than the sunset, more tempting than any siren of the sea, more precious than any gem in a treasure trove, loving how his name sounded on her lips. "But another kiss wouldn't hurt anything."

"No." Her lips hovered centimeters from his mouth, her breath warm, inviting, making him want more than she was willing to give. "One more kiss wouldn't hurt, Vale. But just one more because I won't be one of your girls. We aren't having a weekend fling or rumble between your sheets or whatever you want to call it."

"Okay," he agreed, breathing in her warm, vanilla scent, so clean and refreshing, like her. "Just one more kiss because you aren't one of my girls and don't want to be a rumble between my sheets this weekend."

He continued to tell himself once more while he kissed Faith reverently, his hands cupping her face, his fingers partially threaded into her pulled-up hair, his gaze locked with hers.

The kiss was gentle, searching, desperate and yet lingering as if they had all the time in the world to explore each other's lips. It was a kiss unlike any Vale had ever experienced.

A kiss that made him wonder what else with Faith would be like nothing he'd ever experienced.

That wonder both thrilled him and scared the living hell out of him.

Feeling like a plucked chicken in a room full of swans, Faith sat in the upstairs media room with the women staying at the Wakefields' Cape May mansion. Sharon, Angela, two of Sharon's college friends, Vale's other cousin Monica, and Steve's younger sister, Francis Woodard. Vale's mother and Sharon's parents had retired to bed around ten, claiming they were too tired to sit up with the younger women and reminding Sharon to be sure to get her beauty sleep so she wouldn't have bags under her eyes.

The men had gone out for drinks and Steve's bachelor party, Vale included. Each second that ticked by brought his return closer. And when he returned they'd be expected to share a bedroom. Did Vale sleep in pajamas? Or would he slide between the sheets in nothing more than he'd brought into the world?

"Tell us," Francis cried after downing a shot of something bright red and grabbing Faith's hand, pulling her from her meanderings. "What's it like, dating Very Scrumptious Vale?"

She didn't want to lie, but what could she say? "Mostly, we just work together."

"Honey, we all saw that kiss down on the beach." Francis fanned her face with exaggeration. "If you were on the clock, sign me up for medical school."

Faith's face burned. Okay, so the groom's little sister had a point. But how did she explain what she didn't understand herself?

"It's complicated."

"Love always is," Sharon sighed.

"We're not in love," Faith quickly denied, unwilling to perpetuate the misconception.

"I saw the way Vale looks at you." At Faith's raised eyebrow, Sharon went on. "He looked at you as if you're the only woman in the world, as if he would have liked to push you down in the sand and made love to you right there, the world be damned." She smiled, taking on a dreamy look. "I know love. It's exactly the same way Steve looks at me."

"You're mistaken." Vale had looked at her with lust because she was convenient, because they were at a wedding and people did stupid things at weddings. Like get married and believe in happily ever after.

"I know Vale," Sharon boasted. "He wants you."

Yes, he'd told her that. And, truth was, just having Vale desire her was so much more than she'd ever dreamed possible. So why had she said no?

He hadn't said the words out loud, but essentially he'd been asking her to have an affair with him. A fling that would last the weekend and be done when they left the magic of the beach.

But she couldn't say yes, not when she'd be expected to work side by side with him as if nothing had happened.

Lord, how was she going to work with him night after late night now that she knew his kisses tasted of ambrosia?

"Oh," Sharon cooed, "you're in love with him, aren't you?"

Faith opened her mouth, ready to deny his cousin's claim, but nothing came out. Nothing at all, because she didn't know how she felt about Vale. Not any more. From before they'd met, she'd admired him professionally, had known she wanted to work with him, had used every resource within her repertoire to arrange an interview. When they'd met, she'd been thunderstruck by emotion so potent the magnitude had almost blinded her.

She admired Vale, professionally and personally, although she'd hesitate to admit the latter to anyone other than herself. Physically she wanted him, but what heterosexual woman wouldn't?

This weekend she had the opportunity to be with him and was too scared to accept the risk that chance would change everything between them. Bok. Bok.

Only sometimes change was inevitable, and inevitably her relationship with Vale had undergone a change she couldn't undo even if she wanted to.

Taking that chance would strip her soul bare, would let him see into her heart, and therein lay the problem.

She didn't want to give Vale that power over her future. Didn't want to become her mother, settling for whoever came along because she'd tasted love and couldn't hold on to it, forever searching to feed a hunger that couldn't be satisfied.

No, she didn't love Vale and would never, ever allow herself to be that foolish.

CHAPTER FIVE

FAITH tossed and turned in the enormous bed in the giant bedroom their suitcases had been placed in. How could she sleep when eventually Vale would return? Would be sleeping in the same room? Possibly crawl between the sheets beside her if she didn't stay awake and order him to the sofa?

Although his family had been nothing but kind to her, she'd had a difficult time relaxing. How could she fit in when their conversation ran from spending the month in Europe at their favorite French resort to having their thighs liposuctioned in Beverly Hills?

Which should only serve as yet another reminder of why she shouldn't become involved with Vale this weekend. Despite how dedicated he was to his career, to finding a treatment or, better yet, a cure for Parkinson's, the reality was he moved in a different world from that she did.

A jiggle of the doorhandle had her breath catching. Vale.

Peeking through barely open eyes, she took in the outline of his sleek body in the doorframe. So beautiful. So tempting.

Softly, he closed the door, walked over to the sofa and sank down onto the leather. She could feel his gaze on her, could feel his presence so overwhelmingly that she swore the room pulsed with him. His scent. His aura. His heartbeat.

Forcing her breathing to remain even, she closed her eyes completely, feigning sleep. She couldn't deal with him. Not tonight. Not if she didn't want to do something she might regret.

Might, because she wasn't sure.

Perhaps not doing something would be more regrettable than taking action?

She just didn't know, didn't have the experience to know, and for that reason she'd pretend to be asleep to avoid having to act.

"Faith?" he whispered, almost as if he knew she was faking.

She didn't answer and after a few moments he sighed, but didn't call her bluff.

Instead, he disappeared into the en suite bathroom, returned, and slid between the sheets. Next to her.

Would it give away that she was awake if she piled pillows between them? Or if she peeked under the covers to see what he was wearing? *Or not wearing?*

She swallowed, fighting to breathe, fighting to keep her eyes closed in case he was looking at her and could see her through the sliver of moonlight breaking the darkness, fighting to keep from scooting next to him, spooning her body to his.

Because, really, if she did that while still feigning sleep, what would it hurt? She could always plead that she'd gotten cold. Which didn't explain the droplets of sweat forming between her breasts.

She bit the inside of her lower lip, forced herself to count sheep, to count the soft sounds of Vale's even breathing. That he'd crawled into bed and fallen immediately to sleep didn't say much about her effect on him, did it? He was in bed with her for the first time ever and had immediately dozed off.

The last time she recalled taking a peek at him soft streaks of sunrise had started filtering into the room. His dark head lay against the pillow, his lashes fanned out across his cheeks, his face relaxed in sleep.

Unable to resist, she reached out, brushed her fingertip across his cheek, marveling at the smooth perfection of his skin, at how her heart raced at the contact.

Without his expression changing in the slightest to indicate he'd awakened, his hand caught hers, clasped it to him. Faith watched his face for some sign she'd woken him, but none was forthcoming. Neither was escaping his death grip, so she relaxed, cherishing the contact of their skin.

Her hand cradled in his, she finally drifted off into dream-filled sleep.

With the sun streaming into the room through the magnificent windows, Faith woke very aware that she was in Vale's king-size bed that smelled of his spicy aftershave.

She opened her eyes, startled to find the bed empty.

Only the imprint on the pillow next to hers told the tale that he'd shared the bed, that she wasn't imagining his musky scent. Unable to resist, she reached out, touched where his head had lain, calling herself every kind of stupid.

She'd touched him during the night. Had he woken up and known of her foolishness? God, she hoped not.

Slowly, she became more aware of her surroundings. She'd been too restless the night before to fully appreciate the bedroom suite.

Double glass doors led out onto a balcony that ran the length of the room. Pale blue walls with clean lines were broken only by the huge windows and a gorgeous seaside painting. Wow. A panoramic view of the ocean took her breath, easily visible even while lying in the bed. A two-sided glass fireplace divided the room, separating a living area with a sofa and television from the bed area. A couple of medical magazines cluttered the solid mahogany end table. To the far end of the living area a desk with a

state-of-the-art computer was set up. A yellow
legal pad had notes scribbled on the top page in
Vale's distinctive penmanship. Had he worked
this morning before leaving the room?

This wasn't a guest suite. This was Vale's
room. If she walked to the closet, his clothes
would be hanging there. Those had been his personal items in the en suite bathroom, which was
bigger than her entire apartment, and not because he'd brought them from home. No wonder
he hadn't carried more than his small overnight
bag, so sharply contrasting with her large suitcase. He hadn't had to.

But what she didn't see in the room was Vale.
Where was he? Had he wakened, taken one look
at her, and been frightened away? Probably, she
mused. As much as she'd tossed and turned prior
to his arrival in the bed, she imagined her hair
was every which way.

Stretching, Faith decided she'd get up, shower,
and go in search of her host. Only before she'd
so much as lowered her arms the door opened
and Vale entered, carrying a tray full of break-

fast goodies that had her stomach growling in appreciation.

"Good morning, sunshine," he greeted her, fully dressed in khaki slacks that hugged his narrow hips, a white button-down with the sleeves rolled up on his tanned forearms and a sexy V exposing where the top two buttons were undone at his neck.

He'd been the one out partying all night so it was totally unfair that he looked marvelous, and she suddenly recalled the fact she'd just woken up, looked horrendous with not a speck of her new make-up, and her hair wild as Friday evening rush-hour traffic.

She winced, fighting the urge to try to tame the messy strands about her head. No doubt she looked like Medusa with hair snaking about her head in every direction.

"Good morning, yourself." She scooted up in the bed, only to become conscious of her pajamas. During her shopping spree she hadn't considered sleepwear, had never dreamed she and Vale would be thrown into the same room by his mother. She didn't expect her fuzzy *Star*

Wars pajama bottoms and T-shirt top to start any fires.

Hold up. Did she want to start fires? Hadn't she told herself time and again while lying in his bed last night that she needed to keep distance between them this weekend if she didn't want to destroy her career? If she made love with Vale, no way could she continue to work with him when he moved on to another woman. To do so would be torture of the cruelest kind.

She considered herself a modern woman, but she didn't do casual sex. She didn't do sex at all.

She flopped back on her pillow with a sleepy sigh.

"Not a morning person?" he teased, placing the tray on the bed. "I brought you breakfast."

She glanced down at the tray. Fresh fruit, yogurt, bagels with peanut butter, juice, milk, a pot of coffee, and…she lifted a metal lid off a plate…eggs, bacon, sausage links, and toast with butter and jelly.

"You don't really expect me to eat all this?"

His gaze raked down her bare arms, instantly covering her with goose-bumps of awareness.

She was in his bed. Could he see how her nipples strained toward him? She hoped not.

"Wouldn't hurt you if you did," he assured her, "but I thought you might share."

Not waiting for her to respond, he climbed into the bed beside her. Faith grabbed for the tray, certain the contents would topple, but it didn't budge. What kind of mattress was this anyway? A very expensive one, she decided, trying to ignore Vale's long frame stretched out beside her, fluffing pillows behind his back. Trying to ignore that now every cell in her body strained toward him as if she were metal and he the most powerful of magnets.

Mr. Magnetism pulled back a plastic wrap and spread cream cheese on a bagel, offering the pastry to her. "Have fun with the girls last night?"

Reaching for the bagel, she nodded. "You have a lovely family, Vale."

"Lovely?" He curled his nose, preparing a plate of food for himself. "They've snookered you."

"And you?" she asked, popping a bite of the

bagel into her mouth. "Did you have fun with the boys, doing all those wild bachelor party things men do?"

She'd meant her question to be teasing, casual, but when he turned to her there was nothing teasing in his eyes, nothing casual in the way her heart mimicked a space-shuttle launch.

"I'd rather have been with you."

Vale watched Faith's eyes darken to a deep green at his admission. He wasn't accustomed to things spouting out of his mouth that he hadn't planned to say. But his words were true.

He would much rather have been here with Faith than at Steve's bachelor party.

Several of the groom's football buddies had apparently thrown him a huge bachelor party in Philadelphia the weekend before so last night's had been more about tradition than one last yahoo on the town.

The entire time Vale had wondered what Faith was doing, how she was getting on with his family.

He wondered that a lot these days. He'd be sitting at home and would glance at his watch and wonder if she'd still be awake and, if so, what she was doing. Sometimes he wondered if Faith wasn't why he worked so many hours, just so he'd have an excuse to see her.

Which was crazy. If he wanted to see her outside work, all he had to do was ask her out.

But something in the way her green eyes darkened and her bagel stopped halfway to her mouth told him maybe that wasn't all he had to do.

Which was perhaps why he'd never asked her out.

That and the fact she had a bright career ahead of her at the clinic and didn't need personal issues muddying the waters. He didn't need personal issues muddying the waters. Other women were disposable in his life, but he enjoyed working with Faith. Enjoyed the constant she provided.

"Was Steve's party not a success?" Her gaze didn't quite meet his.

"Bachelor parties aren't my thing." Did she have any idea how beautiful she was this morning? He'd wondered about her hair—now he knew. The long tousled-from-sleep golden strands looked like extensions of the sunbeams streaming in through the windows, casting a halo around her angelic face.

Her eyes were huge, her lips full, her face naturally classic. He'd never wanted to brush his fingers over a woman's skin more. Never wanted to tangle his fingers in a woman's hair more. Never wanted to kiss a woman more.

Never wanted to be inside a woman more.

Which was why he should climb out of the bed just as he'd done after lying next to her for a couple of hours, unable to sleep for the temptation of her sweet vanilla fragrance and warm body. He'd not slept a wink and had known he wasn't going to with her lying next to him. Still, he'd lain next to her, knowing she was feigning sleep and wondering why she bothered, wondered why he himself bothered. Had she thought he'd force her into something she didn't want? That he'd seduce his way beneath those awful fuzzy pajamas she wore?

When she'd touched his face, he'd thought he imagined the light touch and had instinctively clasped her hand. Lying in his bed, holding Faith's hand, had felt right, but had left him throbbing with need. After she'd gone to sleep properly, he'd risen, logged into his computer, and gotten some work done, all the while distracted by Faith in his bed and by how much he wanted to wake her with his mouth, his hands, his body over hers, moving in hers.

"Is there anything about weddings you like?" she asked, apparently oblivious to where his thoughts had gone. Or purposely ignoring that he was likely looking at her as if he'd like to have her for breakfast.

"Open bar?"

"Besides the free booze?" She popped the torn-off piece of bagel into her mouth and he envied the food.

"The cake?" Why was he imagining that pink tongue of hers licking frosting from her lips? His tongue cleaning a spot she missed?

Her gaze met his. "Be serious."

"I am." He seriously wanted to push her back on his bed and settle between her thighs and *seriously* make her orgasm over and over.

"No, you're not."

She thought not? He shrugged. "I imagine the honeymoons aren't bad."

She rolled her eyes. "You would think that."

"You asked." He picked up a strawberry and placed the fruit on her plump lips.

Her pupils dilated as she stared at him with a "What are you doing?" expression, but she took a bite of the berry, wiping at the juice that covered her lips. "Thank you."

"You're welcome." His pants shrunk around him, restraining him. What would she do if he really did push her back on the bed, stripped those hideous pajamas off her, and ran his tongue over her, tracing a path to her core and dipping inside?

"What are you doing, Vale?"

His gaze shot to hers, saw the uncertainty shining in her eyes. "What do you mean?"

"This." She spread her arm toward the tray. "I'm your colleague, not your girlfriend. You shouldn't be serving me breakfast in bed or feeding me strawberries. This is crazy."

"This weekend, for all intents and purposes, you are my girl."

"Vale…" She took a deep breath, swallowed. "I won't be used just because I'm convenient."

Convenient? "You think I want to make love to you because you're convenient?"

"Let's be real here, Vale. We've known each other for months and you've not exactly had to hold yourself back to keep from ripping my clothes off."

He couldn't deny her claim. Yet… "You're different from the other women in my life, Faith. You have been from the beginning."

"Because I'm one of the few women under forty you haven't jumped into bed with," she pointed out with a snort that didn't come across as being quite natural.

"Actually…" he gestured to where they were "…I have jumped into bed with you, but that isn't the point."

She regarded him with obvious frustration and confusion. "Just how many women have you jumped into bed with that you haven't had sex with?"

"None," he answered immediately.

"One," she corrected, picking up a strawberry and biting into the juicy flesh.

"Yet." Because he was damned sure he was going to make love to her soon. Today. Never had he wanted a woman so much. But he shouldn't make love to her. Deep in the recesses of his brain, he knew he should keep his hands off Faith.

"I thought we decided to end this madness last night with the kiss on the beach? That our having sex would ruin our professional relationship?"

"Tell me, Faith, when you closed your eyes last night, did memories of that kiss fill your head as you drifted to sleep? Did you dream about me waking you with my hands on your body, my mouth on yours?"

"No."

But she was lying. That was why she'd touched his face, his lips. She'd been wondering what them making love would be like.

"When I came in here last night, found you in my bed, I wanted to strip you naked and make love to you. Good thing you were asleep or I might have."

With a guilty wince, she averted her gaze. "You were drunk."

"If I'd been drunk, we'd be having a morning after." Stone-cold sober, it had taken all his willpower not to pull her to him and kiss away any objection she made.

"A morning after where you reminded me that sex with you means nothing?" Her brow lifted accusingly. "That I'm nothing more than a quick rumble between your sheets which I've already told you I refuse to be?"

Was that what he'd be telling Faith if they'd had sex? It was what he'd be reminding any other woman of, what he'd have stressed long before they'd got to the bedroom. Yet the thought of telling Faith that she meant nothing to him other than mutual physical satisfaction didn't sit well with his conscience.

Yet he didn't want more than mutual physical satisfaction with any woman. Not even Faith. Just look at how his few relationship attempts had ended when he'd involved more than his body. Not good and not something he'd repeat.

"I don't know the answers to your question, Faith," he answered honestly, struggling with his conflicting desires where Faith was concerned. "Like I said, you aren't like other women."

"Because I work for you?"

"Maybe." He enjoyed working with her, enjoyed the sharp way her mind tackled problems, came up with innovative solutions, the way her eyes lit up when they operated successfully, when they discovered a new abnormal neuronal pathway trend on the brain maps Brainiac Codex generated on their Parkinson patients.

"I like my job, Vale. A weekend romp with you isn't worth destroying my career or placing myself in a position where I'd be forced to relocate."

That said it all. A weekend romp wasn't worth losing his relationship with her either. Was that why he'd let her feign sleep when he'd wanted nothing more than to spread her legs and lose himself? They'd said as much the night before but, having spent the night tormented with being so close to her yet so far away, he'd lost sight of that. Something he couldn't allow himself to do. Otherwise he'd seduce Faith before the weekend ended, and then where would they be?

Other than blissfully sexually satisfied, that was?

Faith could easily have felt like a fifth wheel with all the wedding activities. Between Vale's constant attention and his family including her as if she'd been a part of the family for eons, only the occasional doubt plagued her. Sharon Wakefield had been a doll, more genuine and kind than Faith would have believed possible of someone so physically flawless.

Most of the day had been planned to a T, but not long after lunch Faith had time on her hands and a heart longing to walk on the beach. She wore white Capris, a silky green top the sales clerk had said perfectly matched her eyes, and sandals she could easily kick off for a beach walk.

First telling Virginia that she was going to take a walk, Faith weaved her way through the flowers, chairs, and wedding regalia, to head down the path toward the water.

Once barefoot on the sand, she opted to head in the opposite direction from the one she and Vale had taken the night before. She'd had enough problems keeping her mind off him today without reminders of that kiss. A long walk on the beach would do her good, would help clear her mind so she could think straight.

"Hey, wait up."

On hearing Vale's voice, she bit back both a sigh of appreciation and a wince at not having the much-needed break from his overwhelming appeal.

"I thought Sharon needed you?" She waited while he rolled up his pants to mid-calf, exposing the sprinkling of dark hair covering his legs. Faith gulped back another sigh, staring down at his bent head. Sunshine glistened off the natural lights in his thick locks, off the flexed muscles in his neck.

He glanced up, caught her watching him, and grinned. "Sharon can get by without me for a few minutes. She has everyone else jumping to her tune."

"It's her wedding day. Everyone should be jumping to her tune. Besides, you don't have to entertain me 24/7," she responded, resuming her walk along the edge of the water. "I'm a big girl and can take a walk on the beach by myself."

"I know you can, but humor me. I've had about all the wedding I can stand and the ceremony hasn't even begun yet."

That, Faith understood. For a few brief moments every now and again she got caught up in Sharon's excitement, forgot how much she detested weddings, but most of the time that same old pain gnawed in her belly.

"I'm no more a fan of weddings than you are."

"Because of your mother?" He fell into step beside her.

"I suppose." She didn't want to talk about her mother and her many weddings. Not on the beach with Vale on the day of his cousin's wedding. The only wedding Faith had agreed to attend other than her mother's. She'd refused every single invitation from friends, had pleaded out of the weddings of two med-school friends who'd asked her to be a bridesmaid. Yet Vale had convinced her to come this weekend without too much cajoling. Why was that?

"How many husbands has she had?"

Why did he always push when she wanted him to leave a subject alone?

"John's her sixth." She stepped into the oncoming wave nipping at her feet.

"Ouch."

"Yes, ouch." And not the cold Atlantic water rushing around her ankles, although that had definitely bitten. "It's difficult to watch her make the same mistakes over and over."

Having stopped beside her, he considered her answer. "They're her mistakes to make."

"True, but you'd think she'd eventually learn."

"Maybe she's just lonely."

"A person doesn't have to get married to abate loneliness. She could have gotten a dog, you know."

His expression became thoughtful and he asked a bit too casually, "Like Yoda?"

She spun toward him. "Yoda is my best friend and not because I'm lonely. Far from it."

Had she sounded defensive? What was she saying? She *was* defensive.

"A dog is your best friend?"

"Obviously you've never had a dog or you wouldn't ask that question." She glared at him. Of course he wouldn't understand. How could he? He'd probably never been lonely a day in his life and if he ever was, all he had to do was crook his sexy little finger and women would come running to do his bidding.

Not that she was lonely. She so wasn't.

"You're right," he admitted, meeting her glare head on. "I've never had a dog. I always wanted one while I was growing up, but Mom's allergic to pet dander."

"Poor little rich kid."

One side of his mouth lifted in a half-smile. "I'm not going to get any sympathy from you, am I?"

"No." She turned back, gestured to the mansion still easily visible in the distance. "That's your house, Vale. Not even your main house, but your East Coast beach house. It looks more like a modern-day castle."

"That's my mother's house. Not mine. I live in a Manhattan condominium."

"In a building your family owns." She took a deep breath, gave him her pretty-as-you-please smile. "Besides, the room where we slept, that's your room."

"How do you know?"

As if she could not know. "You're stamped all over the place."

He chuckled. "I'm what?"

"The medical magazines, the toiletries in the bathroom." She resumed walking away from the house. "I don't know specifically what it is, just that the room looks like you."

"I look like a bedroom?"

Oh, yeah, she looked at him and saw a big bed. With their naked bodies twined together. He looked like sex. Sex she couldn't have. Not with him, and she'd never wanted sex with anyone else. Why did he have to be the one to make her body come alive? Why him? A rich playboy who was her boss and frustrated her so much?

"Let's change the subject," she ground out, wanting to hit him for the mess he'd made of her emotions. She'd been able to keep her attraction to him neatly tucked away until this weekend.

Why had he had to push her into coming when she'd known she shouldn't?

Faith hadn't thought it possible that she'd doze off when Vale had ordered her to lie down for a nap—a nap!—while he showered. But her lack of sleep from the night before and the beach air must have been working on her because when she opened her eyes after what she'd thought had only been a few minutes, he had finished showering and was gone.

He'd left a note on the bedside table, saying he'd see her at the wedding but wouldn't likely come back to the room prior to the ceremony.

She glanced at her watch. Wow. She'd slept for almost two hours. She'd better get started or she'd be late.

Donning the dress she'd instantly known was "the one" when she'd seen it in the shop, she zipped the side zipper, loving the body-hugging shape of the emerald-colored dress with its flounced hemline.

Usually she dressed to blend in with her surroundings. As a woman competing in what many still considered a man's world, she'd always felt the need to tamp down her sexuality. Not today.

Today, she wanted to feel all woman.

Today, she did feel all woman.

Because of Vale and the way he kept looking at her.

She still wanted to pinch herself that he wanted her, that she was the one holding back on them having a weekend fling.

She had no doubt he was telling the truth when he said he wanted to have sex with her. Part of her thrilled that even that was possible after a year and a half of him seeing her as a sexless colleague.

But she knew his attraction was circumstantial. That he'd want to sleep with any halfway attractive woman he'd brought with him this weekend. It wasn't her specifically he wanted. Just that he was a highly sexual man and she was a young, healthy woman. Of course his hormones would be kicking in. She didn't fool herself that him wanting her could possibly mean more.

If she even slightly let herself believe him wanting her meant more, she'd be a goner.

Imitating the style the hairdresser had done the day before, Faith loosely piled her hair on top of her head, securing the strands with a rhinestone comb. She brushed make-up across her cheekbones, accented her eyes, painted and glossed her lips until she looked like a perpetual pouter.

When she'd finished, she stood back, surveying her handiwork. Not bad. Not enough to erase the first scary image of her that morning that was probably forever imprinted on Vale's brain, but not bad.

She made her way down one of the matching curved staircases, careful not to disturb the white silk ribbon and flowers tied to the handrail.

People were everywhere. Caterers, wedding guests, more family members and friends she only recognized from having seen their photos in magazines. What was she, Faith Fogarty, doing here in this paparazzi orgy?

Following the trail of people, she made her way to the back of the house, reminding herself with each step that she was a successful neurologist and she was here because Vale wanted her here. The patio area had been decorated with hundreds of white flowers and miles of white silk ribbon. Beyond the gated pool, a pristine white carpet ran the length of the rows of chairs to where the gazebo had been laced with white gardenias, vivid green leaves, and ribbon. The sun slowly beginning its descent toward the ocean provided the perfect backdrop.

If she wasn't so anti-weddings, she might think Sharon's wedding beautiful. Oh, who was she kidding? This was a beautiful wedding. Just as her mother's weddings had all been beautiful.

Just that, like the beauty of the sunset, none of the marriages lasted.

Where was the beauty of putting all your hopes and dreams in another person only to have those hopes and dreams trampled on?

Would Sharon's wedding last? With her mega-wealth and role as former Miss Pennsylvania, she was a celebrity, just as her professional footballer husband was. The odds were against them even before they made their vows.

"You look absolutely stunning but, then, my son has superb taste," Vale's mother interrupted her thoughts, meeting Faith at the back of the chairs. "Come with me. The family is sitting up front."

Faith blinked at the woman wearing a designer dress that probably cost more than she made in a year. "I'm not family."

"Nonsense." Virginia smiled at her. "You're here with Vale. That makes you family."

Touched by the woman's continued unexpected generosity, Faith followed her to one of the front aisles and sat down. "Do you treat all Vale's guests so warmly?"

His mother's blue gaze, so similar to his, met Faith's. "If you're referring to the women in his life, he's never brought a *guest* to a family function. You're the first and only."

A warning went off in Faith's head, leaving her feeling dizzy and unsure of what she'd thought she'd known about him. "Vale's never… But…"

His mother laughed at her astounded expres-

sion. "I know my son is no saint. I see the pic-
tures of him with all those women. But family
functions aren't a place for him to bring some
woman he's passing time with. He knows that.
That's why we were all so excited when he said
he was bringing you."

And Vale thought bringing her was going to
protect him from his family? Hello, he'd created
a whole new range of problems by bringing her.

"B-but we work t-together," she stammered,
still digesting the news that Vale didn't bring
women home. None of the beauties he wined or
dined had ever slept in the big bed occupying
his suite in the beach house. Just her.

"Which explains why my son works so much."
Her eyes twinkling with delight, Virginia patted
Faith's hand. "You don't have to explain your
relationship with Vale to me. Just know that I'm
happy you're here. We all are because it's been
so long since Vale's let down those shields of
his."

Faith wanted to crawl under the seat at the
hopeful anticipation in his mother's eyes. Besides, what was she referring to? Vale's shields?

That made it sound as if Vale had once had his heart broken. Had he? It seemed a strange thought. Faith couldn't imagine any woman not falling under Vale's spell. The man was a hypnotist, a wizard of wondrous proportions when it came to wielding power over the opposite sex.

"Vale and I really are more friends."

His mother's penciled on brows rose in perfect arches. "Are you saying I'm wrong? That you're not in love with my son?"

She studied her so intently Faith closed her eyes, took a deep breath. "You're not wrong."

Faith swallowed. Hard. Had she really just said she loved Vale? She didn't. *Did she?* Sure, she was fascinated by him, admired him, wanted him. What sane woman didn't? But love? Did such a fanciful emotion even exist?

Dear Lord. He was a hypnotist and she'd fallen completely under his spell this weekend.

"Good." Virginia squeezed her hand. "Now, let's sit back and enjoy this wedding we've been planning for years. I can't believe our little Sharon is all grown up and getting married."

Faith couldn't figure out how to politely

remove her hand from Vale's mother's so she left it. Seconds later the groom and his men came to stand at the gazebo and Faith could only stare at Vale, in awe at how handsome he looked in his tuxedo, how tall and confident, how he completely outshone the groom and every other man who'd ever lived.

He took her breath away in his black and white tuxedo. Somewhere in the time since she'd last seen him he'd had a haircut and fresh shave. He came to a stop in his designated place, his hands clasped in front of him, his eyes immediately searching out hers.

When he spotted her, his gaze lingered on hers a moment, then raked over her, taking in her appearance, appreciation glimmering in his eyes when they returned to hers.

"You're beautiful," he mouthed, obviously not caring who saw.

Faith blushed, feeling as if she'd just won the lottery.

"So are you," she whispered back, wondering if he'd be able to read her lips, if he'd see how much she wanted him at that moment, how no one existed for her except him.

One corner of his mouth lifted in a pleased grin and he winked.

Faith's brain went fuzzy and she couldn't breathe.

A tight squeeze of her hand had her breaking away from Vale's gaze to stare half-unseeing at his mother.

"Looks as if we'll be planning another wedding by Christmas," she said excitedly, smiling at Faith.

Another wedding?

"Not my wedding. Uh-uh. No way." She shook her head, knowing that, regardless of how Vale made her feel, she didn't want to marry him. Never, ever would she set herself up for that kind of failure, that kind of disappointment. Having watched her mother's heart break time and again, Faith would never go through that. Never. "I don't want to get married to Vale, or any other man."

Virginia frowned, but didn't have a chance to comment as the small orchestra set up along the back of the yard began to play. Bridesmaid after bridesmaid walked up the rose-petal-strewn carpet until the wedding march sounded.

Everyone in the crowd stood, turned to see the bride in all her spectacular glory.

Faith was sure Sharon made a beautiful bride, but her vision had clouded over and she saw another wedding, another bride. Although she tried to choke them back, tears streamed down her cheeks now as they had then. Tears of pain and sorrow. Tears of loss. Tears of knowing her heart would never be complete again.

Her mother's wedding.

The first of several that had followed over the years.

She never wanted to be like her mother. Yet wasn't she?

Tears flowed at the realization she wasn't so dissimilar after all, despite years of walking a straight and narrow path, putting her education, her career before all else. Still, she'd foolishly done as her mother had, doomed herself to wanting a man she'd never really have. Vale.

"Here's a tissue, dear." Virginia pushed a clean

but wadded tissue paper into her hand. "I came prepared as I always cry at weddings too."

Embarrassed that she was weeping at a virtual stranger's wedding, Faith took the tissue, knowing nothing would dry the tears that would flow when Vale broke her heart, as he inevitably would.

Because if he really wanted her he'd have her before the weekend ended and there was nothing she could do to stop him unless she left right this very moment.

CHAPTER SIX

How many photos did one need at a wedding? Too many, Vale decided a half-hour after the ceremony had ended and the photographer was still imitating a general on the battlefield. Forcing yet another smile, he held his pose.

He'd had enough and just wanted to go find Faith to see if she was okay.

When the rest of the guests had been looking at Sharon walking down the aisle toward her groom, Vale had been watching Faith, noticed she'd only half turned, had seen the tears in her eyes.

Not tears of joy over the bride-to-be's happiness, but tears of sorrow and pain. Tears that alluded to past hurts.

Instinctively he knew Faith's hang-up with weddings had to do with her mother, probably to do with her numerous weddings. Faith had admitted as much without telling him any real details. He'd wanted to ditch his role in the wedding and go to her, comfort her, take her in his arms and kiss her until she never cried again.

Had his mother not turned, handed Faith the tissue, not patted her hand in comfort, not reminded him with a quick meeting of the eyes that he had a duty to Sharon not to ruin her special day, maybe he would have. He certainly hadn't been thinking of his cousin when he'd spotted Faith's tears.

All he'd been thinking about had been the woman he couldn't stop thinking about, the woman he'd watched sleep, wondering what it was about her that fascinated him so. He'd known she was hurting and he'd wanted to go to her.

How had his mother known to turn, to catch him watching Faith, to see his inner turmoil over her tears?

Maybe a mother just knew. His certainly always had.

"I've had enough," he announced to no one

in particular. "Any other photos requiring my presence will have to be taken later."

The photographer must have been finished with him anyway because no one seemed to mind when he left the wedding party to find Faith.

The guests had been served a sit-down meal and Faith had to be at one of the long white tables dotted across the lawn or inside the tent. But he didn't spot her. Not even with his mother, which is where he expected to find Faith.

His mother's gaze shifted purposefully toward the house and he sent her a silent "Thank you".

She wasn't downstairs, so he headed up to his suite.

"Faith?" he called when he entered his room, not seeing her in the sitting area. When he turned toward the bathroom she was coming out, another tissue in her hand. Some of her hair had worked loose from its upswept style. Her nose was red and her eyes puffy. Her make-up was slightly smudged.

"What are you doing in here?" she asked, looking at him in confusion. "Aren't you needed for photos?"

He couldn't move, could only stare at her and wonder at the pangs in his chest. "You've been crying."

She winced, wiping at her eyes as if that would somehow disguise the truth from him. "It's nothing. Weddings make me cry, that's all."

She was a horrible liar and unaccustomed guilt hit him.

"I shouldn't have made you come with me this weekend. You told me you didn't like weddings and I didn't listen."

She forced a small smile. "It's okay, Vale. I need to get over my phobia about weddings. Besides, you needed me to protect you from your mother's matchmaking."

Rubbish, he thought. He could handle his mother. Sure, she'd been hinting more and more for him to find someone to share his life with, telling him he worked too much, needed to enjoy life, and had paraded female after female in his path the last time he'd visited. Having Faith at his side had ensured she wouldn't do that, making his weekend less complicated. Only perhaps having Faith at his side had complicated things in ways he wouldn't be able to easily undo. Regardless, at the moment all he wanted was to protect her, to take away her pain and promise her everything would be okay.

Whatever the everything that had upset her was.

Was he right and it had to do with her mother or was her phobia something more personal? Had Faith been engaged in the past? Married even?

His chest pang grew stronger.

"I wanted you with me, Faith." He pulled her into his arms and she willingly went, laying her head against his tuxedo and wrapping her arms around his waist. The pang clawed at his throat, threatening to give him heartburn. "But it was unfair of me to force you to come to something that obviously distresses you so much. I'm sorry."

In all the time Faith had known Vale she'd never heard him say he was sorry. Not that he was the type of man who thought he was too good to do so, just that he was rarely wrong. Maybe never.

"It really is okay, Vale," she breathed against his chest, loving the strength she found in his arms, loving how tightly he held her, as if he planned to hold her for ever. "I wanted to be with you this weekend, too."

Now, that was really stupid. Why was she telling him that? The next thing she'd be blurting out that she was in love with him. She wasn't in love with him. This wasn't love.

"I mean…" Oh, what did she mean? With him holding her, she couldn't think and her mind had already been cloudy from her cry-fest. Silly that weddings made her sad, made her miss her father, made her wonder if she'd been responsible for him leaving, and if she was doomed to repeat her mother's mistakes.

"I don't know what I mean, Vale. I'm so confused about everything this weekend. Weddings confuse me. You confuse me. The way I want you, yet I know I shouldn't." There she went, saying stupid things again. "I can't seem to think about anything but you, Vale. Make it go away."

He tilted her chin, stared into her eyes, then did what she wanted more than anything, what she'd been waiting for nearly a lifetime. He kissed her with all the passion of a man who wanted a woman intensely. With all the gentleness of someone who cared about her and didn't want her to hurt, who really did want her pain to go away. He kissed her with all the fierceness of a man who wouldn't be denied, a man used to conquering the world.

Faith kissed him back with matching passion, gentleness, and fierceness, but also with everything in her heart, knowing that he alone could take away the ache in her chest, that only he could make her feel whole.

Was that love? Was that what she was feeling for him?

She couldn't think of that now. Not while he was touching her.

He trailed kisses over her exposed neck, onto her bare shoulders. Cupping her bottom, he held her to his groin, pressing her into where he'd grown hard for her.

For her.

Because he wanted her.

And she wanted him.

For once she wasn't going to deny herself a guilty pleasure, wasn't going to deny herself what she'd likely spend every day of the rest of her life regretting.

She'd regret not making love to Vale more. Lots more.

She kissed his throat, tugging on his bow-tie to loosen the material so she'd have better access to his body. She kissed the open V of his tanned chest when he tossed the tie to the floor, undoing the top couple of buttons. She continued to kiss him while her fingers worked the remainder of his buttons loose and pushed his shirt open, exposing the ripped planes of his abdomen.

"You have a beautiful body," she praised. A gorgeous body that looked more like it belonged on a pin-up poster than a physician.

"Isn't that my line?" A half laugh, half groan sounded from deep in his chest, changing to a full-blown moan when she bent and kissed his flat belly.

"Faith," he growled from beneath clenched

teeth, "you'd better know what you're doing because my willpower is almost gone. Has been
almost gone from the moment I spotted you at
the wedding. I wanted to ditch the ceremony and
carry you up here, spend the night making love
to you."

He'd thought all that when he'd looked at her?
When he'd told her she was beautiful?

She rubbed her cheek across the sculpted
planes of his lower abdomen, loving his indrawn
breath, how he pulled her to his mouth, pressing
a kiss to her lips.

"Much more of that and I'm going to push you
back against my bed and make you mine," he
breathed against her mouth. His fingers bit into
her bottom, grinding her against him. His gaze
held hers, branding her with his hot desire. "All
mine. Be sure this is what you want or stop me
now because I want you."

Did he intend his words to deter her? Because
if he was almost gone, she was all the way. Gone
out of her mind with need and longing and the
desire to feel wanted, loved, to be enough for

someone. To be Vale's whole world, even if for just a few moments in time.

Rather than heed caution, she slid her hands beneath the open flaps of his shirt and pushed the material off his shoulders, letting her fingers trace over the taut muscles. "I don't want your reason, Vale. I want you to make love to me."

"Faith." His eyes deep blue seas, he shrugged out of his shirt and claimed her lips again. He feasted on her mouth, drawing out every morsel of pleasure within her, making her tingle from head to toe in sheer awareness of her very being.

She wound her arms around his neck, ran her fingers through the short hair at his nape, held him to her.

Not that she needed to hang on to him.

Vale wasn't going anywhere. He wanted, needed, as much as she did. His fingers had worked up her skirt, bunching the clingy material at her waist, revealing the garter and thigh-highs she'd bought to go beneath her dress.

"Faith," he hissed against her mouth, leaning from her long enough to take in her new sexy undergarments. "You're killing me."

She might have felt embarrassed except for the raw desire shining in his eyes. No way could she want to do anything except stand in the glow of his gaze when he looked at her as if he'd just awakened on Christmas morning and found exactly what he wanted beneath his tree. Her.

Thank God she'd listened to the saleslady and bought new underwear to go with her weekend wardrobe. The scraps of silk and lace had been worth every high-priced penny.

"Faith," he repeated, tugging her back to him, his groin thrusting hard against her belly, his hands everywhere on her body. "I want you so much."

She'd have told him to take her, but he was kissing her again, so she told him with her mouth, her hands, her body, with every fiber of her being.

She lowered his zipper, sliding his pants down his thighs and marveling at his body, at his reaction to her every touch, marveling at her boldness with his body.

She freed him, encircling him with her hands,

stroking over the silky smooth skin. He was big, hard, jutting out proudly toward her, magnificently male, but she wouldn't have expected anything less. Not from Vale.

When his fingers pushed aside her lacy panties, rubbed across where her every single nerve ending culminated into one tiny nub, she cried out his name.

"You like that?" he asked, although surely he knew the answer as her body moved in rhythm to his touch, moved as if she were a puppet he controlled.

"Please," she whimpered.

Please don't stop.

Sliding one finger then another inside her, he stroked until she could stand no more, until she was on the verge of shattering, until her legs turned to jelly. She was thankful he held her, otherwise she'd be a puddle of hot liquid on the floor.

"You're so tight."

"Vale, I need you inside me." Please. Please. *"Oh, please,"* she pleaded against his neck, amazed by the warm waves washing through her, amazed that he was holding her, touching her, wanting her, amazed at the foreign sensations swamping her body. Her head dropped forward, resting in the crook of his neck as each cell in her body performed acrobatics, pulsating toward him in sweet, gratifying throbs of pleasure. "Vale!"

First donning a condom, he gave a satisfied growl, looped his hands beneath her bottom, lifted her legs to wrap around his waist, to press against where he'd created the most fabulous magic inside her. He backed her against the bedroom wall, using the sheetrock to help support her, to help keep her in position. She didn't stop him. Not when the full length of him glided against her, testing her moist readiness. Not when the thick head of him pushed inside, making her breath catch in her throat, stretching her beyond belief.

"Vale!" she gasped at the same moment his eyes widened with horrified realization, at the same moment every muscle in his body tensed.

"Faith..." He sounded tortured, seemed to

hate that his hips moved in automatic response to her tight pelvic muscles, even when he was hurting her. She could feel his restraint oozing from every pore of his body, could feel that he barely held on to his control as he gently stroked within her. Yet hold on to his control he did in slow, methodical flexing of his hips that tormented as much as pleased her.

She didn't want his control. She wanted him filling her, making her a woman, his woman. She wanted him thrusting against her, hard, wild, as out of control as her heart.

She squeezed him between her thighs, gyrating her pelvis, wanting him to re-create the magic his fingers had spread through her earlier, wanting him to forget his control, to forget everything except the coming together of their bodies in unfettered passion.

"Faith," he groaned, sweat beading on his forehead. He stared into her eyes, his breaths coming hard. "You have to stop. I can't— I don't want to hurt you."

"Then love me," she urged, opening her body

to him, opening her heart to him. She gripped his shoulders, stared into his eyes, letting him see everything she felt for him, hugged him tightly with her inner thighs, drawing him as deeply into her body as she could. "Love me now because I need you, Vale. I need you so badly. Please."

His pupils darkened, his eyes growing feral at her plea. His lips covered hers, smashing her mouth, thrusting his tongue into the deepest recesses as he lost the battle he'd been waging and slammed his body into hers with primal need beyond his control.

A battle Faith was glad he lost, because in him doing so she won.

Won the most glorious of colors bursting through her.

Won the hottest heat, the moistest heat, a heat that burned her the whole way through, scorching her skin, searing her insides.

Just when she thought she'd reached the pinnacle of sensation overload, she fell.

Into mindless oblivion.

Mindless orgasmic pleasure.

Further emotionally tangled with the man she clung to in hope of not floating off into another dimension.

Vale wondered whether anyone would notice if he failed to show back up at the reception. Because what he wanted was to carry Faith over to the bed and make love to her properly.

Not with her dress bunched at her waist, not with his pants sagging to his ankles. Not with him so out of control that he'd taken her like a savage beast when she'd been a virgin.

A virgin.

He'd just taken Faith's *virginity.*

She'd been right there with him, wanting him as much as he'd wanted her. But he felt a heel all the same. He'd known she was upset, that she'd been crying, that she was vulnerable. He shouldn't have taken advantage of the situation. Not with Faith.

"I shouldn't have done that."

The smile that had been on her lips faded and he felt an even bigger heel.

Her eyes became guarded and she twitched at

his waist, reminding him of all the reasons they shouldn't have done what they'd just done.

What had he done to her? To them? And how the hell was he going to fix it without losing the relationship he'd enjoyed with Faith before the wedding weekend?

CHAPTER SEVEN

"Put me down." Faith pushed against Vale's chest, wanting to stand on her own two feet, wanting to pull her dress down, wanting to be able to think and knowing she couldn't when their bodies were still joined.

Thank heavens he'd used a condom.

Not once had she thought of protection. Stupid and immature and something a teenager might do, but she truly hadn't thought of anything except needing Vale.

So much for being a modern woman.

How much more stupid could she have been?

He stepped back, gently disconnecting their bodies and lowering her to the floor. He held her shoulders a moment until he was certain she was steady on her feet. "Dear God, Faith, why didn't you tell me you were a virgin?"

His voice held a strangled mix of what sounded like anger and frustration. *Great.*

She tugged her dress over her hips. "What does that matter?"

"It mattered." He ran his fingers through his hair. "I've never done that before."

Wasn't that her line? She glanced at him, grimaced at the regret on his handsome face. "What?"

"Been with a virgin."

"Really?"

He nodded, wiping his hand over his face, before meeting her eyes. "Oh, yeah."

Was it wrong that she liked being the only virgin he'd ever been with? His *first* first?

"I shouldn't have taken your virginity, Faith. Not me. Not like this."

"In case you didn't notice, I wasn't complaining." As much as she'd like to let him shoulder the blame for what she'd likely later classify as a moment of insanity, she couldn't. She'd wanted him, had begged him to make love to her.

"Faith, why were you still a virgin?"

She bit her lower lip and sat down on the end

of the bed, all her happiness gone. This wasn't the conversation a woman wanted following her first sexual experience.

She forced a smile, hoping to recapture the closeness she'd felt to him only minutes before. "Seriously, Vale, it's not that big a deal."

"Apparently it is." He lifted her chin, stared straight into her eyes, and asked a question she didn't want to answer. "Why haven't you had sex with any of your past boyfriends?"

Past boyfriends? Yeah she'd had a few, but she'd never let any get close, never wanted to risk having her heart broken when they packed up and left, as they'd inevitably do.

With Vale she'd only acted on instinct, followed her heart. Which was cause for grave concern. "The timing was always wrong."

"You're almost thirty. You're not going to convince me that 'timing' is why you were still a virgin." His gaze pinned her, not allowing her to look anywhere but into his eyes. "Maybe you'd like to explain what your real reasons are."

Actually, she wouldn't like explaining her reasons at all.

Because then she'd have to admit to him something she hated to admit even to herself. Whereas her mother welcomed men into her life, believed their lies, Faith did the opposite. She'd pushed away the few who'd tried to get close.

Because she was beating them to the punch.

She squeezed her eyes shut, unable to take his probing blue gaze a moment longer.

"Faith?" His voice was gentle, his thumb stroking along her jaw in a tender caress. "Did someone hurt you?"

She kept her eyes closed. "Let it go, Vale."

"Not until you tell me why a woman as beautiful as you opted not to have sex until me."

He wasn't going to drop this. She knew he wasn't. This was Vale. He would keep at her until she told him.

Taking a deep breath, she opened her eyes, glared at him. "Why would I want to have sex with someone who was just going to leave?"

His expression darkened, but his touch remained gentle. "You mean me?"

"I mean men period. All men leave."

"Not all men," he denied, his fingers soft against her cheek.

"Yes, all men." She pulled away, walked across the room to stare out at the ocean. "My own father didn't even stick around. Why would I expect any other man to stay when I wasn't good enough for my own flesh and blood?"

"If your father left, it was because he wasn't good enough for you, Faith. Not the other way around."

Spinning to face him, she rolled her eyes. "Right."

"I'm serious."

"Fine, but you know it's not even just me. It's men and women in general. Men leave. It's what they do best."

His brows knotted together in a V. "How is it that I never knew you were so jaded about the opposite sex?"

"Being logical is not being jaded," she pointed out, moving her head enough to free herself from his hold, but she stuck her ground. "I'm just realistic."

"Right," he mimicked her earlier sarcasm.

"Fine." She shot him a challenging look. "Give me one example of a man who stuck around."

He shrugged. "Easy. My father stuck around, Faith. Until the day he died he loved my mother, was faithful to her. They had a loving and happy relationship."

"Oh? Why don't I see you leaping down the path of love and happy relationships then?"

"That's different."

"How?" This time it was her eyes pinning him into place, his gaze averting. "You have a wonderful family, Vale, and you just said that your parents had a wonderful relationship. Why wouldn't you want the same for yourself?"

His lips compressed into a tight line. "I'm not my parents."

"Meaning?"

"Meaning what they had was rare."

She gave him a "duh" look. "My point exactly."

"Point taken." He grinned wryly. "But times are different from when my parents fell in love. Now women are more concerned with the Wakefield name, the fame and fortune, than they are with the man."

"Shall I say it?" Her brow arched and she gave a snide *"Right"*. Surely he didn't believe it was money and notoriety that made women flock to him? No way. "I've seen how women chase you, cling to you, want to be with you," she reminded him. "Don't fool yourself that it's because of anything other than *you*."

"You might be surprised," he said so sincerely that Faith blinked, took a step back.

"A woman used you for your name in the past? Someone you cared about?" Did she sound as shocked as she was?

"Let's just say that some life lessons are learned the hard way and that's a mistake I won't be repeating." He took a deep breath, glanced around his suite. "Let's straighten up and go back down to the reception."

His admission kept echoing through Faith's mind while she cleaned up in his bathroom, making herself presentable. His words were still echoing through her mind when, hand in hand, they returned downstairs to the reception, which was in full swing and without their absence having been noticed.

Seeing so many happy wedding-goers seemed a slap in the face following the conversation she and Vale had just had.

They stepped into the giant reception tent. The bride and groom had been toasted, had cut the cake and were now sharing their first dance as man and wife. A few other couples had joined them on the parquet dance floor that had been set up beneath the tent.

A photographer immediately snapped a candid picture of Vale and Faith and then requested they pose, which they did. Faith glanced at Vale, wondering if he was upset at them having their photo taken together, but he seemed oblivious. Then again, he was used to having his photo taken.

She, on the other hand, wasn't and felt highly self-conscious of her every move, of every camera flash. Could everyone tell what she and Vale had been doing? Was it stamped across her forehead that she'd just lost her virginity?

Oh, my. She'd just had sex. With Vale. Amazing, glorious sex. With Vale. Vale. Vale. Vale, who some crazy woman had once used and obviously hurt.

She snuck another glance at him.

"Let's dance," he suggested, tugging her toward the dance floor and into his arms as if nothing out of the ordinary had happened between them. As if her mind wasn't racing in a hundred different directions.

She didn't argue, could barely find words to speak at all.

Her first sexual experience hadn't exactly been a romantic coupling but, wow, she and Vale had lit fires.

Fires that still burned low in the pit of her stomach.

Relishing being back in his arms, she let him guide her onto the dance floor, memories assailing her. They'd danced before, at the office's New Year's party. That had been the first time Faith had been in his arms. She'd floated home that night, positive the year was going to be her best ever.

The second time had been after she'd helped perform her first DBS two-lead implantation as

Vale's second. He'd been so proud he'd popped a bottle of champagne that evening, poured her a glass, and he'd toasted her. Just he and she over a working dinner where they discussed the surgery and ways they could improve technique and efficiency.

Always she'd been aware of wanting him, of how desirable he was, of how he made her so aware he was a man and she was a woman. Looking back, she had to wonder about Vale.

Had the chemistry between them been building from the moment they'd met? Had he felt it all along too? Or had it truly just been that they had been thrown together by circumstances this weekend and otherwise what they'd shared would never have happened? That he never would have seen her as anything more than a surgeon in his employ?

"Faith?" he whispered next to her ear, startling her back to reality.

"Hmm?"

"Let's forget about what happened."

Any hope that what they'd shared had been special to him died.

"Okay." What else could she say? No, I don't want to forget what we just shared because it was amazing and I want to experience it again? True, but not appropriate when he was obviously not feeling the same and trying to back out of the corner he'd landed in. "We'll forget what happened."

But she knew she would never forget Vale making love to her. Not ever. Not even when she'd pray to forget in the hope of finding inner peace.

"What I mean…" his hands moved over her back, settling on her shoulders "…is that I want us to have fun tonight, to enjoy each other's company and not focus on what we did."

"Fun. Right."

He tilted her chin. "Are you saying I'm no fun?"

She stared into his blue eyes. Maybe he was right. Maybe they did need to forget about what they'd done, even if only for a short while.

"Who, you? The original Mr. Workaholic?" she attempted to tease, but knew her eyes were filled with longing, confusion.

"Hey." He pulled her close, and instantly she was taken back to what they were supposed to be forgetting, "I've barely cracked a patient profile all weekend."

"True, but you've been busy."

"Spending time with you this weekend has been immensely enjoyable."

His body pressed so tightly against hers was immensely enjoyable, too. She couldn't help but smile. "Okay, I concede your point."

The music changed to another slow song and Vale kissed the top of her head, weakening her knees. "Before the night is over, you'll be conceding much more, Faith, because I'm going to make love to you again."

Hadn't they just said they were going to forget what they'd done? Knees knocking, she met his gaze, saw the desire that still burned there, and understood fully what he'd meant. He didn't want the fear of what they'd done and how it would color the future affecting the rest of their weekend together. Their wonderful, magical weekend where they would have fun and enjoy each moment as a man and woman who wanted each other and were free to explore that desire.

And although it went against logic, against what was deeply ingrained in her psyche, Faith's smile widened and she relaxed in his arms with the knowledge that somehow everything really would be okay. She leaned her head against his shoulder, joyful at the feel of his lips at her temple, and let her imagination run wild with thoughts of acceding to Vale's every sexual whim.

Senator Evans's son couldn't be more than seven or eight, but the kid had more energy than a power plant. Unfortunately that worked to his disadvantage when he raced around the reception tent and knocked over a large vase filled with flowers, causing him to let out a blood-curdling scream as the arrangement tumbled down on him.

At the commotion, Vale stopped in mid-sentence in his conversation with the lead singer of an up-and-coming rock band he'd been talking to and rushed to where the boy cried.

Faith beat him to it, though, and was gently examining the little boy she'd knelt next to. "Hi, sweetie, my name is Faith. I'm a doctor and saw that vase attack your head."

The boy just kept his hands over a spot on his head and continued to cry.

"Can I see where the vase hit?" she asked, gently pulling his hands away so she could see.

Vale knelt next to her, ordered a waiter to bring them some ice and to find Senator Evans and his wife.

"Amazingly, there isn't a cut," Faith voiced Vale's thoughts and held her fingers up in front of the boy's face. "Can you tell me how many fingers I'm holding up?"

The boy, whose sobs had begun to abate to just streams of tears running down his smudged face, stared at Faith's fingers and said pitifully, "Two."

"Very good," she praised, giving him a gentle hug. "Can you follow my fingers with your eyes without moving your head?"

The boy nodded and did as she asked as she checked his visual tracking. Vale pulled out his keychain, which had a tiny flashlight on it, and handed it to her so she could check the boy's pupil reflexes.

She did so, smiling and continuing to praise him in a voice that Vale found mesmerizing.

Watching Faith interact with the boy, give him praise and a quick hug, made him want to praise her, hug her. Made him think she'd be a good mother.

She would. Faith put her whole heart into anything she did. The thought of her body round with child, of her giving birth, of seeing her holding a baby, hit him.

He blinked, wondering what was wrong with him, wondering where his crazy thoughts had come from. He didn't want Faith pregnant. *She'd leave him.*

Not him.

She'd leave the clinic, at least for a while, would devote herself to her child, to her child's father.

Which had his throat tightening.

Was it because he knew he was her one and only lover that he felt so possessive? That he didn't like the thought of another man touching her? Impregnating her? That he thought of her as *his*?

She'd been a virgin. A *virgin*. Because she believed no man would stick around for her. And she'd let him be her first, him, a man who never stuck around and had no intention of ever doing so. She deserved better.

Which made the grip on his throat tighten even more.

What was wrong with him? He didn't have thoughts like this. Ever. He shook his head to clear his mind.

"Vale?"

His vision cleared, focused on where Faith stared strangely at him, the young boy now hugged up against her.

"You okay?"

"Fine," he assured, although he wasn't sure of any such thing.

"Here's your light. Thanks." She held the keychain out to him, her fingers brushing his, and desire shot through him again. "Billy doesn't appear to have a concussion. Thank goodness."

Vale looked into her beautiful face, into her eyes, and another wave of possessiveness hit him. A wave of protectiveness.

A wave of something he couldn't recall ever having felt before and honestly couldn't say he liked feeling now.

Panic clawed at him, made him want to high-tail it back to New York, back to his comfortable relationship with Faith. But memories of her saying that leaving was what men did, of the hurt in her eyes when she'd commented on her father, had him standing his ground. So he smiled at the vulnerable woman responsible for the odd feelings in his chest and reached for her hand, lifted it to his lips.

"You're an amazing woman. I'm glad you're here with me."

Her brows drew together in confusion, but then a smile spread across her lovely face and he was glad he'd resisted the urge to run, because for the rest of the weekend he was going to indulge in heaven.

"Me, too."

* * *

Had Sharon's bouquet toss been rigged? When Vale's cousin had turned, winked at Faith, she'd suspected, had tried to step back, not wanting to catch the flowers. But the throng of women had pushed her forward, preventing her escape. The bouquet practically jumped into her hands, making her wonder if Steve had been teaching Sharon passing secrets. Instinctively Faith had closed her fingers around the flowers.

If for the right reasons, none of which involved marriage, though, she could be very happy with Vale. At least tucked away in this magical world of Cape May where he only had eyes for her, she believed she could. In the real world, he'd eventually move on to greener pastures and break her heart. But during their fantasy weekend she could forget the real world existed and pretend she could have a happily-ever-after of her own.

"What are you thinking?" he asked, leaning in to where she sat at one of the decorated tables, sipping a glass of water. She'd had all the champagne she could handle earlier—a mere two sips.

Three and she might be dragging Vale beneath a table.

"That I didn't want to catch this." She gestured to the flowers on the table. "Sharon purposely tossed me the bouquet."

"You think?" He was grinning still, which eased the tension ebbing through her. He didn't believe she was trying to push him into anything. Good, because she wasn't.

"Okay, so the wink gave her away," Faith admitted.

He took her hand in his and studied their clasped fingers. "My family likes you."

"What's not to like?" She mimicked words she'd heard him say on numerous occasions.

His gaze lifting to hers, Vale laughed. "Have phenomenal sex with a woman and it goes to her head each and every time."

"Really?" she asked, searching his eyes for a hint at how he felt. How he really felt about what had happened beyond the *phenomenal sex*. "You've had this happen before?"

His expression grew serious. "Nothing like you has ever happened to me."

"Because you'd never been with a virgin before?" Why was she pushing? Did she really even want to know the answer?

"I don't know."

What else would there be different about her compared to every other woman he'd known? Other than a brain? Vale was brilliant, gorgeous, successful, and as rich as sin. He had his pick of women and, despite whatever had happened in his past, he was never in short supply.

Except as wedding dates. For that he'd chosen someone who knew him well enough to know he had no desire to settle down, someone he himself had said wasn't a real date.

"If not that, then what?" she asked, unable not to push, unable not to try to glean better insight as to how he felt about what she'd classify as the most earth-shattering experience of her life.

"The not being able to stop even when my brain told me to," he clarified. "I only hope I didn't hurt you too badly."

"You didn't." At his raised eyebrow, she relented. "Okay, you hurt at first, but only for a few seconds, Vale. Then it was wonderful. Perfect."

He shook his head. "Not perfect. You're first time shouldn't have been against a wall with our clothes still on."

Puh-leeze. She couldn't imagine a more perfect experience. He'd been consumed with wanting her.

"I'm not complaining."

His gaze swept over her, caressing each feature. "You should be."

She drank in the warmth of his expression, the desire in his eyes, and realized she wielded a feminine power previously unrecognized. "If I was complaining?"

His gaze darkened and he lifted her hand to his lips, pressing a kiss to her fingers. "I'd have to do my best to make amends for my lack of finesse as your first lover."

"Do your best?" Excited shivers shot through her body, congregating at the juncture of her thighs. "As in?"

"Take you to my bed and show you just how good sex can be."

"It gets better than this afternoon?" She found that difficult to believe. He'd been amazing. More than amazing.

His gaze not leaving hers, he nodded. "Much better."

"Vale," she began in her most serious voice.

"Hmm?" he played along, his fingers tracing over her bare arm, leaving a path of goosebumps dotting her skin.

"About this afternoon…" She brushed her foot against his calf, dipping her toes under his pants cuff. "I have a complaint…"

His eyes not leaving hers, he stood, lifting her to her feet along with him as if she weighed nothing. "Let's go."

She glanced around at the reception still in full swing, despite the bride and groom having left earlier for a surprise destination. "Don't we need to say good night or something?"

"Good night or something," Vale mocked, clasping her hand tighter. He walked up the steps that led to the patio and pool, not stopping until they were in the house, up the stairs, and in his room.

CHAPTER EIGHT

"Now, tell me about that complaint." Vale shut his bedroom door, locked it, and turned to the woman who was driving him crazy.

Crazy with lust.

He wanted her again.

As much as he had this evening.

As if he hadn't already had her rough and ready against his bedroom wall. Just the memory had him groaning with desire, groaning with need to plunge inside her again, over and over as deep as he'd go until he spilt himself deep in her belly.

That thought had him pulling his wallet from his tuxedo jacket, removing a foil packet and tossing it onto the nightstand. There was a box in his shaving kit but that would require a trip into the bathroom. A trip he'd make later because once more wasn't going to be enough.

He hadn't stopped wanting Faith. Another first for him. Never had he not been satiated with sex. Never had he been left wanting round two before they'd even made it out of the bedroom after round one. If not for his love for his cousin, he'd never have left his suite. Not for the rest of the weekend.

He wanted round two with Faith *now*.

If he wasn't careful, he'd lose control again. No, he wouldn't. He refused to hurt her again. He'd make love to her, gently, relishing her body and teasing her senses to highs so grand she'd think she'd left earth.

"Vale?" She took a step backward, but her eyes danced with mischief, danced with excitement at their flirtatious play. "You're making me nervous."

He took a menacing step toward her. "You'll like it better."

"Promise?" A smile curved her full lips, lit her eyes, sucker-punched him in the gut.

How was it possible to want her so much?

"Oh, yes." He advanced on her, closing the gap she'd created between them. "I promise you'll like what I'm going to do to you. You're going to like it a lot and beg for more."

Vale set about making his point, proving that he was a man of his word.

By her whimpers of pleasure he would say he was right. Faith enjoyed every single touch, kiss, lick, suck, thrust.

She moaned her delight, matched his passion, tested his willpower beyond what he thought he could endure. Somehow he managed not to lose his control, not like he had that first time, never like that again, not until she'd thrown back her head, arched off the bed, and screamed his name.

Then he allowed himself to let go, to lose himself inside the sweet escape she so generously offered.

Faith was in no rush to leave Cape May. Maybe she wanted to stay for ever, just stay wrapped in the exquisite cocoon of Vale's undivided attention.

Unfortunately Sunday morning arrived all too quickly. She and Vale were sitting on his private balcony, having breakfast that had appeared while she had been in the shower, letting the hot water ease the subtle aches in her muscles. She stared out at the ocean waves.

Cape May was a place of magic. No, the amazing man sitting across from her was the real magic.

"Could we walk on the beach before leaving?" she asked, wanting to prolong the fantasy as long as she could. She didn't need him to spell it out for her to know that everything would change once they were back in New York.

Vale would be back in his zone, would have the world at his fingertips. She'd go back to being his neurologist in the operating room, jumping to his every command.

Only she hadn't quite figured out how she was going to convince her body that she was no longer allowed to ignite from just looking at him. It had been bad enough prior to the having made love.

Now that she had experienced the wealth of his knowledge, she wasn't sure she had the strength to deny how her body danced to the music of his touch. She didn't fool herself otherwise, that somehow she was different from every other woman Vale had cast his spell over.

His gaze went out to the ocean.

"Most of my family is still here," he mused, taking a sip of his juice. "Now that the wedding is over, they'll be anxious to start plotting their next big event." His face wrinkled with displeasure. "I'd rather not be around for that."

His meaning dawned on her. "You think they'll be plotting about us?"

He finished off his glass of juice. "You caught Sharon's bouquet. Of course they'll be plotting. To no avail, but they'll be plotting."

To no avail. There it was. A reminder that they weren't a couple and nothing had really changed between them. He was her boss. She was his employee. When they returned to the office, they'd pretend they hadn't kissed every inch of each other's bodies. At least, she'd try.

Vale no doubt had enough experience with weekend-afters that going back to the norm would be no problem.

He leaned across the table, brushed his finger

at the corner of her mouth. Ack! Had she had a crumb on her face? He just smiled. "But if you're not in a rush to return to the city, we could drive to the lighthouse."

His unexpected offer caught her off guard, had her gaze shooting to his. "The lighthouse?"

Faith had barely set foot outside Manhattan and had never had the time or money for tourist stops. "I've never seen a lighthouse in real life."

"Never?" His brow rose. "That settles our plans for the day, then. We'll drive to the state park where the Cape May lighthouse is located, and go up."

Delight filled her. "We can go up it?"

"All the way to the top," he said in a teasing tone. "A hundred and ninety-nine steps."

She gave him a quizzical look. "A hundred and ninety-nine steps? You know that how?"

"I'm a brain surgeon. I know everything," he teased.

With an eye roll, she smiled. "Of course you do."

He just grinned. "When I was a little boy I

climbed to the top of those steps and had the T-shirt to prove it."

"I bet you were a cute little boy."

He waggled his brows. "I'm a cute big boy, too."

"That you are," she agreed, loving that he was smiling at her, whatever had been weighing on his mind apparently pushed aside. For the time being, at any rate. "That you are."

Virginia Wakefield hugged them both goodbye, promising to call for lunch the next time she was in Manhattan. Faith just hugged the woman back, accepting a kiss to her cheek, wondering why she wanted to burst into tears at the kindness Vale's family had extended toward her. She followed him to the car where he stowed her suitcase.

Lost in thoughts of the weekend's events, she truly hadn't been prepared for her first sighting of the lighthouse above the tall grass blowing back and forth along the roadside.

"Wow." She strained her neck, trying to keep the red top in her line of vision.

"We're almost there," he promised, turning the car down a winding, tree-lined road.

"We can really go to the top?" she asked again, not quite believing that she was looking at a real-life lighthouse. "Is that something anyone can do or just a Wakefield?"

"You think I get special privileges?"

"I know you do."

He chuckled. "For a few bucks anyone can go to the top, but it is a good hike up the stairs. You up to it?" He shot her a quick glance, his gaze dancing over her with obvious intent. "After last night you might be too sore to climb stairs." His grin was lazy, wicked, full of hot, steamy seduction. "I seem to recall you swearing you weren't going to get out of bed today."

Yeah, she had sworn that. She'd slept very little, instead reveling in the fact she lay cradled in Vale's arms, her cheek against his strong chest, listening to his heartbeat.

"Good thing I'm a girl who likes a challenge."

He'd definitely challenged her. Time and again. Over and over. Guiding her through wave after sweet wave of pleasure. Just the memory of him maneuvering her onto him, his hands cupping her hip bones, guiding her, her back arched just so, angling her against him until she'd shattered. Completely and thoroughly *shattered.* She'd collapsed onto his chest, smiling, gasping for breath, amazed at how he'd played her body like a master musician, making her sing his praises, cry out his name. Just remembering had her squirming against the soft leather of the passenger seat, wanting him yet again.

Knowing if she didn't get her thoughts under control she was going to forget the lighthouse and climb into his lap instead of up the steps, she shifted her gaze out the car window. "The lighthouse is magnificent, isn't it?"

Vale parked the car in the lot between the lighthouse and the bird sanctuary also located in the park. A wooden boardwalk led down to the beach. Beyond that, she could hear the Atlantic crash into the shore.

"Yes." Vale's voice was low, husky.

Her gaze shot to his. She swallowed hard at what she saw glimmering in his azure eyes.

Lust. Hot, sweaty, climb-into-my-lap-right-now-and-use-me-for-your-pleasure lust. Oh, my!

An elderly couple with binoculars walked past the car, bursting their sensual cocoon, reminding them both they sat in a public parking area. Faith sucked in a deep breath, wondering if she had the strength to climb the stairs after all. Her legs had turned to jelly.

"Let's go." Vale raked his fingers through his hair, cleared his throat. He opened her car door and extended his hand. He didn't let go as they crossed the parking lot. "Cape May's a functional lighthouse, a means of saving ships from crashing against the shore. The coastguard maintains the lights."

They walked to the base, entered the building just inside the gate of the fencing around the lighthouse, and bought two tickets. The usual touristy type gifts were also on sale. T-shirts, postcards, snow globes, and keychains. Faith picked up an inexpensive snow globe with the lighthouse inside, fluffy specs of white drifting around when she turned it upside down.

When she set the globe back on the shelf, Vale

pulled out his wallet. He handed the trinket back to her. "I want to give you a keepsake of today."

Swallowing the emotion clogging her throat, she nodded, knowing she'd treasure the globe for ever. While she waited at the base of the lighthouse, chatting with the lady inside, Vale returned to the car and stowed her snow globe.

Step by step they climbed to the top of the tower. They paused at each of the five small landings, reading the history of the lighthouse. Their privacy was only broken by two young women and their giggling daughters' descent. Faith smiled at the girls' delight in counting each spiraling step in a sing-song manner. She didn't want kids, but those two were cute and the women's smiles made her just a touch envious. Which was ridiculous. She was there with Vale. They should be the envious ones. With the way the blonde's gaze flickered over Vale, perhaps they were.

No wonder. The man was multiple orgasms just waiting to happen. Faith sucked in a breath, clenched her thighs, and willed her body to quit throbbing.

Vale greeted the worker who sat at the top by name, shook his hand, and bent to say something to him. The leathery-faced senior glanced her way, nodded, and left. Truly alone, they went out to the barred railing hand in hand.

"I can't believe I'm here. With you," she admitted when she stepped out onto the roost.

The wind whipped at her hair and a fear of heights she hadn't known she possessed tugged at her belly, leaving her a little dizzy. Or maybe the fact all her blood pulsed down south was why her head spun. With her free hand, she grasped the handrail running against the exterior of the lighthouse. They walked to the far side, looked out over the ocean, having a bird's-eye view of the sanctuary and surrounding property.

"Beautiful," she gasped. "Absolutely beautiful."

"Yes, you are. Come on." He tugged on her hand. "Let's make our way around and check out the views from up here."

"Wish I had a camera," she mused minutes later, staring out over the ocean, "but experiencing picture-worthy moments is really what life's about."

Something she'd not done up to this point in her life.

She'd been living inside a cage of her own making. A huge city-size cage, but a cage all the same. A cage she hadn't realized until experiencing a weekend with Vale.

"You have a way of seeing things in a unique light, Faith."

If he only knew.

She leaned against the red bars protecting her from falling, gazing at the ground below, reeled at the beauty of the coastline.

Vale's hands clasped her waist, pulling her against him.

"What?" She turned, pressed her hands flat against his chest, confused by his sudden motion, wanting him more than she should.

He kissed her. Right there at the top of the lighthouse. Any dizziness that might have been from heights was replaced by the mind-numbing dizziness his kisses carried.

"I've always wanted to do that," he admitted in a low tone, holding her close.

"Kiss a girl at the top of a lighthouse? Is that why you got rid of that man?"

"Kiss a beautiful woman at the top of this lighthouse and, yes, I asked Ray to give us some privacy."

Wrapping her arms around his neck, she threaded her fingers through the hair at his nape, wondering what he'd say if she told him she wanted him.

"I want you," he told her against her lips, molding her body to him.

Yep, she couldn't miss that. Not with his body fitted so tightly to hers. He kissed her again, his hands cupping her bottom, keeping her pelvis ground against him. Not that Faith needed any encouragement. Most likely this was the last time she'd get to experience Vale like this, to taste his lips.

Definitely the last time because anything more and she might fall into some fantasy world where she believed she and Vale had a chance, might end up like her mother down the road. No, she'd take this moment, make the most of it, and then she'd go on with her life. It was what she wanted. What Vale wanted. Everything would be okay.

Desperation flowed through her veins, making her crazed, making her crave him with an addict's fervency. Maybe he felt crazed as well. His hands caressed her everywhere, his mouth marauded hers with demanding kisses, his body moved against hers.

When he tugged on her skirt, lifting the material, sliding his fingers beneath the lace of her panties, Faith moaned.

"Vale," she breathed, vaguely recalling that they stood at the top of a lighthouse

"Shh, no one can see us," he assured her. "And even if they can, they can't tell what we're doing. We're too high up."

Which didn't really reassure her, but his flinger flicked across where she throbbed, and all sane thought disappeared in the pleasurable fog that followed. His gaze locked with hers, he brought her to orgasm, smiled with satisfaction when she melted against him.

"You first. Now it's my turn." With that, he

spun her and was inside her in the space of a breath. Hard, fast, deep, he thrust, stopping only long enough to swear and don a condom, before plunging back into her in a climactic finish.

Trying to catch the breath he'd stolen, Faith let go of the railing, turned and placed her hand on his cheek. His skin was warm beneath her palm, smooth and spicy from where he'd shaved that morning, moist from where he'd just made love to her.

She stared into his eyes, the intense blue shaming the sky around them. Her chest threatened to explode with the emotions she felt for this man. She could only imagine the outpouring of her love beaming out the top, lighting up the world with a kaleidoscope of colors. Vale's world. The brightness of her love a guide to lead him safely home, to her. For ever.

Oh, Lord. What was wrong with her? She'd gone all sappy. For ever? For ever didn't exist. Not outside fairy-tales and romance novels.

"Faith." Her name came out a breathy sigh and he closed the gap between their mouths, brushing his lips across hers in a soft, reverent kiss, then pulled back to stare into her eyes.

Could he see the truth? Could he tell how much she wished this day would never end? That they could go on inside this magical beach bubble for ever? A bubble where just the two of them existed in this magnificent world?

Lord, her thoughts had gone corny. She wasn't some silly schoolgirl prone to fantasies. She was a highly skilled neurologist, logical, realistic.

"We should go," she insisted, pulling away from him. Their weekend was almost over. It was time for her to get back on track with life, with what was important. Her career. "I need to get back to the city."

Back to reality.

His pupils dilated, and he watched her as he straightened his clothes. "If that's what you want."

She nodded, but felt a sharp jab when he turned without another word, without meeting her eyes. In that moment she knew that to Vale she was merely another woman he'd spent an enjoyable weekend with.

They'd had a weekend together. No strings attached. And that was all she wanted. Really.

CHAPTER NINE

VALE stared at the heavy traffic impeding him from putting his pedal to the metal the way he longed to do. Anything to abate this sense of unease weaving its way through him.

Faith was shutting him out.

The drive back to the city had grown more and more tense as blue skies had transformed into Northern New Jersey gray smog. Silently, they'd crossed over the Hudson and back to reality.

She'd not said a word to him. If he asked a question, she gave a short, almost snippy response. Had he hurt her at the lighthouse?

No, he knew he hadn't. Not physically.

Emotionally? God, he hoped not. He'd made her no promises, had only been acting on the intense attraction between them. He never made promises to women. Hadn't he learned better than that years ago?

Plus, there was the added complication of he and Faith working together. An affair between them would jeopardize the easygoing relationship they'd always shared.

But the reality was he'd be willing to continue his relationship with Faith. Willing? More like he didn't know how he was going to be near her without touching her. Without wanting to hear his name on her lips.

Had she seen that in his eyes? Was that why she'd pulled away from him? Why she'd begun to shut him out?

Because she was afraid that if they continued it would have an impact on her career?

He pulled up outside her building.

"Just let me out so you don't have to park."

"Parking isn't a problem," he assured her as he turned into the parking garage. "Besides, I'll get your suitcase."

Turning to stare out the passenger window as if she was looking at the most amazing sights rather than the boring concrete of the parking garage, she went back to ignoring him.

Vale had had enough. "Talk to me, Faith."

She didn't look at him. Only the stiffening of her spine gave a hint that she'd even heard him.

"Faith?"

She sighed. "What do you want me to say?"

"Tell me what you're thinking. What you're feeling."

"That going with you this weekend was a big mistake."

"We don't have to end with the weekend, Faith." Had he really just offered to have a relationship with Faith? A real relationship where emotions were on the line? Where they would exclusively see each other? Where they would share much more than their bodies? Hell, they already did share much more than their bodies.

She spun in her seat to face him. "That would be an even bigger mistake."

He parked the car, turned off the ignition. "Why?" Not that he couldn't name a hundred different reasons. Not that he could believe he was trying to convince a woman to have a relationship with him. Women chased him, not the other way around.

"Why?" she scoffed. "Because I'm not the kind of woman you date."

She had a point. He'd never dated anyone like Faith. Had never even met anyone like her.

"Maybe you should be."

"I'm not changing into one of those arm-candy girls." Her retort bordered on snide.

"That's not what I meant, Faith." He raked his fingers through his hair, searched for the right words, words that wouldn't leave his lips easily as they lowered the shields he'd painstakingly erected so long ago. "I meant maybe I should be dating women like you. Specifically, I should be dating *you*."

"Why?"

Why? Was she kidding? He frowned. "After this weekend you have to ask why I want to date you?"

She waved her hand dismissively. "That was just sex."

"Really? Just sex?" He'd had sex before. Whatever had happened between Faith and himself had never happened before, though. He'd never felt that protectiveness, never lost reason. Just the memory of being inside her was enough to make his brain cloudy. "I thought it was more."

Her green eyes narrowed, her jaw dropped a bit, and she regarded him quizzically, before laughing a bit hysterically. "Oh, I get it. You're worried that because I was a virgin I'm going to have all these great expectations of you. Don't worry, Vale. The only expectation I have is for us to continue our working relationship as if this weekend never happened."

A strange pain shot across his chest. "You don't want to see where whatever this is between us could go?"

"I know where it would go. Nowhere. And I'm not willing to mess up my career to go nowhere."

Her words stung, yet he recognized the validity of what she said. Still, he played devil's advocate. "How can you be sure we wouldn't end up making my family very happy by making an announcement of our own?"

She snorted. "Because that's one announcement I'll never be making. Never."

He wrapped both hands around his steering-wheel, squeezed the leather. "You wouldn't marry me?"

"I wouldn't marry any man."

"Because of your mother?"

"Because I don't want to be married."

"Fine, I have no intention of marrying anyway, so we're on the same wavelength." So why did her blatant rejection bite so deeply? Why did it make him want to wrap her in his arms and love away the pain she associated with weddings because of her father's abandonment? "Invite me to stay the night."

Her answer was immediate and confident. "No."

"You want me as much as I want you." Was he saying the words for her benefit or his ego's? "I know you do."

She shook her head. "That's just my autonomic neuro-physical response to you. I imagine now that I've had sex I'll respond that way to any attractive male."

What a load of garbage. "Because of your hang-up about your father leaving you, you won't have sex with me again?"

Her face paled and he regretted his sharp question, wondered why he didn't just get her bag out and drive away, never looking back.

"What would be the point?" she finally asked. "Other than a whole lot of pleasure?"

"There are other women who can give you pleasure. Lots of them. This weekend shouldn't have happened. Let's forget it did and go back to just being work colleagues." Her lips compressed into a fine, stubborn line.

He stared straight into her big green eyes, held her gaze, and fought all the warring emotions within him. "That's what you want, Faith? What you really want? For us to forget about what happened and go back to just working together?"

She hesitated only the briefest of seconds, then nodded.

"Fine." His pride kicked in, reminding him that he was Vale Wakefield and had never begged any woman for her attention, for her affections. He sure as hell wouldn't start now. "You're right. There would be no point to pursuing a relationship between us. No point at all."

* * *

Monday morning arrived bright and early, just as it always had. Faith had slept little the night before, despite how tired she'd felt when she'd crawled into her bed. Alone.

No, not alone. Yoda had snuggled next to her, grateful his mistress was home.

But Faith had felt more alone than she had in a long time. Perhaps since her father had walked out on her and her mother.

She knew why.

She'd missed Vale. Two nights in bed with a man should not leave her feeling so lonely. Yet she'd curled into a fetal position and cried. Cried. She'd been the one to tell him to leave, so why had she cried?

Because somewhere during the weekend, when she'd been telling herself over and over that she was no different from any of the other women who'd fallen for him, she'd started to believe that maybe he could someday love her.

And when he'd looked at her at the lighthouse, she'd seen such sweet emotion in his eyes. And that had scared her.

Vale wanted a relationship for however long

those sweet emotions lasted, but how could she do that? Because ultimately he would leave her and then where would she be? Just look at how two nights in bed with the man had messed with her head.

She'd had to face facts that she and Vale had to end things before she forgot to protect her heart, before she got so tangled up in the magic that was him that she lost herself, before she ended up like her mother, chasing an elusive dream of happily-ever-after that simply didn't exist.

Now she had to go and face Vale.

How would he act? Would he acknowledge the hot sex they'd shared or would he go about business as usual?

After her shower, she donned a gray suit that felt shapeless after her Friday shopping spree, scraped back her hair. Unfortunately, with her recent trim, strands kept working loose and she couldn't capture her usual no-nonsense look. Finally, she gave up and twisted her hair in a looser style, securing it with the comb she'd used over the weekend.

Staring at her clean face, she considered slathering on a protective coating of make-up. But if she did, Vale might read too much into it. Much better to go as usual than to have him think she regretted not continuing their weekend. She even made a point to wear her glasses instead of her contact lenses.

Although she need not have worried.

Vale wasn't at the office when she arrived.

"He called to say he had a meeting at the hospital and would see you in the operating room," Kay informed her, handing Faith a stack of papers. "He also asked for you to handle any of these phone calls that you can, to save him time this afternoon. He's got a full day ahead."

Didn't they always? Faith sighed. "Of course."

Kay gestured to Faith's hair. "I like your hair like that. Did you have it highlighted at your appointment on Friday?"

So much had happened between this morning and last Friday Faith had forgotten her co-workers hadn't seen the changes she'd made. "Cut and highlighted. I couldn't get it pulled back right this morning."

"If right is how you usually wear your hair, then good. I like you better this way," Kay said in her usual blunt manner. "How was the grandiose Steve Woodard and Sharon Wakefield wedding?"

"Grandiose," Faith said, not wanting to be reminded of how she'd spent her weekend. In bed, naked, with her boss.

And he'd wanted to continue… If she'd said yes, would she have woken in his arms? Shared breakfast with him? Walked to work with him hand in hand?

No, she'd been right to end things now. Why wait for the inevitable? Why give Vale the chance to break her heart? A relationship between them would never have worked.

"I saw photos in *The Post*. There's a really nice one of you and Vale. You looked gorgeous, by the way, and happy."

There had been photos of her and Vale in *The Post*? What had the caption read? *Wakefield heir goes slumming? Wakefield heir dumps top model for smart chick, what was he thinking? Wake-*

field heir... Faith winced, hoping Kay didn't read too much into the reaction.

Of course there had been photos of the wedding. No doubt gossip rags and papers alike would have a whole section on the famous heiress's wedding to a sporting legend.

"Did you get to meet many stars?"

"A few," she answered honestly. Almost every guest in attendance had had a recognizable face. "Vale kept me pretty busy."

And how. Faith fought to keep heat from her face.

"The man is a workaholic!" Kay accused, but with admiration in her voice. "Well, I hope you got a chance to sightsee. Cape May is a gorgeous historic town. I love all those old Victorian houses. Was the Wakefield home close enough to the park for you to see the lighthouse? I visited there once when I was a kid."

Faith didn't wince again, barely. She even managed a half-smile. "I did get to visit the lighthouse. Thanks for asking." She held up the stack of papers Kay had handed her. "Guess I'd better get started clearing these before meeting His

Highness in the O.R. to implant Mr. Anderson's two-lead DBS device. Keep your fingers crossed we cure his dyskinesia and tremors today without any negative side effects."

When Faith arrived, Vale was already scrubbed and preparing to enter the surgical suite. She hadn't intentionally dawdled, but time had slipped away from her while fielding his phone calls and catching up on her own workload.

"Did Kay give you my message?" he asked, glancing briefly at her when she'd finished scrubbing.

"She gave me all of your messages. I was able to take care of most of them." Did she sound bitter? Ridiculous. She'd been helping Vale from the moment she'd started at the clinic. Why would doing so bother her now? But, then, screening his messages wasn't what caused the bitterness in her throat.

"Good." He stepped into the sterile gown, allowed the nurse to do up the back, then gloved up. Except for the rare comment regarding their patient, he ignored Faith throughout the remainder of the surgery.

Never had he ignored her. Never. Today, he was making a statement. One she was getting loud and clear.

There was no going back to the way things had been before their weekend together.

Unlike her, he looked as if he'd slept well. His appearance was impeccable, as always. No dark circles beneath his brilliant blue eyes, ever. No glances of longing at the woman he'd made passionate love to all weekend.

How dared he make her want him so badly!

Only, really, what had he done? Had sex with her and told her he wanted to continue their relationship beyond the weekend? How could she hold that against him?

But naive as it might be, she hadn't expected such a drastic change in their professional relationship.

He turned, caught her watching him, met her gaze for the briefest of seconds. He never missed a beat in how he guided the DBS lead under the neuro-physicist's guidance, never looked the slightest moved by the questions she knew she hadn't kept from her face.

Then again, the man was performing brain surgery. One wrong move and their patient could have lasting effects. She should be grateful his concentration was on the patient because for once her mind kept veering off track. Not good. Her career was everything to her.

Her guarantee to never fall into the same pitfalls as her mother, to never need a man.

Her gaze shifted to Vale yet again. She didn't need him. Want him, yes. Of course she wanted him. He was gorgeous, successful, brilliant Vale Wakefield. But want and need were two very different things.

Thank goodness she didn't need him, or any man.

No doubt that would hurt even more than the sharp twinges she kept experiencing in her chest just looking at him caused.

Knowing she had to get her feelings safely tucked away, Faith took a deep breath and focused on what she'd focused on her entire life, the one thing she had control over.

Her career.

* * *

"Well done, Vale," Faith congratulated him when they stepped outside the surgical suite. "The DBS implantation went superbly."

Hearing her say his name brought back memories of the weekend when she'd called out his name in sexual release.

Memories he didn't want because what had happened between them had ended with the weekend. What happened in Cape May stayed in Cape May.

Unfortunately.

"We won't really know how successful the implantation was for a few days." Did he sound embittered? Fine. Let her deal with his moodiness.

He hadn't been ready to call quits to their affair. It had been years since a woman had ended a relationship with him. He'd forgotten how much it stung to want someone he couldn't have.

Oh, he could have her. He'd seen how she looked at him this morning. She wanted him whether she wanted to admit it or not. But if he pursued their personal relationship any further, Faith would end up leaving the clinic.

She'd stressed how important her career was to her. What right did he have to screw that up just because he wasn't ready to let go of her delectable body? Just because, even now, looking at her in her hideous glasses and unflattering scrubs, all he could think about was how she'd come alive tangled with his body, how she'd stared at him in wonder at her orgasms, at how she'd looked while sleeping in his arms?

God, he'd missed her last night. Had lain in his big bed alone and wondered why he'd never noticed how quiet and lonely his penthouse was.

Sure, he'd thought of sex from time to time when sleeping alone, but to want to hold a woman, to breathe in her vanilla scent, to sleep knowing she was next to him, would be there when he woke up? *Never.*

Not looking at her, he peeled off his protective gear.

When he turned to go, she touched his shoulder. "Vale?"

Not wanting to, he faced her, but didn't look

into her eyes. He couldn't. Not when he wanted to slide her glasses off her face, lose himself in her gorgeous eyes, and tell her he wasn't willing to let her toss him aside when she so obviously wanted him, too.

"Yes?" He sounded a jerk, but it couldn't be helped. Her gentle touch had electrified his body, had made him acutely aware of how close she stood, of how much he wanted her.

He'd told her he wanted her, that he wanted to continue what they'd started, to see where it took them. She'd been the one to say no. Yet here she was, looking uncertain, hurt. He wasn't going to play games. Did she want him to chase her? To beg her to admit she wanted him? Hell, no.

"I…" She paused, uncertainty darkening her eyes. "Are we going to lunch today?"

Lips held tightly together, he shook his head. "You made your point last week, Faith. Your lunchtime is your own. Unless it's unavoidable, you won't be scheduled for meetings during lunch."

"But—" she began, but he interrupted.

"Don't look a gift horse in the mouth, Faith.

Go, have lunch, and enjoy your free time. I have other plans." He turned to walk away, paused, turned and flashed a grin that was difficult to pull off, but by the paleness of her skin he knew he had, knew he had to drive the point home that either she admitted she wanted him, that she wanted to continue what they'd started, or he would move on. "With Lulu."

He left Faith to stare a hole in his back.

Fortunately, she couldn't see the hole in his chest that hurting her ripped open.

But he wouldn't beg any woman for her affections. Not even one he wanted as much as the one he'd just walked away from.

Three weeks passed. Three weeks in which Faith had barely seen Vale. He hadn't asked her to lunch, hadn't asked her to work late to review the latest data, hadn't asked her input on the Parkinson project. She'd gone from essentially being with him almost constantly to seeing him during roundtable discussions regarding surgical consults and in the surgery suite.

Because he acted as if they were no more than

colleagues. She hadn't expected him to continue to pursue her, but she hadn't expected such a drastic change from their pre-wedding weekend either.

Thank goodness she'd gotten her period, that an unplanned pregnancy hadn't resulted from her weekend of foolish fantasy.

Despite the additional time she had at home with Yoda, time she'd desperately wanted, she wasn't happy, was actually quite miserable.

Was actually quite lonely.

She missed Vale.

All the extra hours she'd put in had never seemed like work because she'd been with him.

Now work was a drudgery. She had to force herself to go in each morning. To know that if she saw Vale, it would only be a glimpse, would only be from a distance, because he avoided her, acted as if she had the plague.

Even Kay commented on the change in the relationship between and Vale, asking Faith if she was okay. Everyone else in the office had either not noticed or failed to comment, probably the latter.

"Faith?" Kay beeped Faith's office. "Sharon Wakefield Woodard is on the phone for you. She called in on Vale's private line. Do you want to take the call or shall I take a message?"

"Faith Fogarty," she said into the phone, confused why Vale's cousin would be calling her. Surely she'd only just returned from her honeymoon?

Sharon didn't bother with pleasantries, actually sounded a bit perturbed. "We need to do lunch."

Do lunch? Faith glanced over her schedule for the day, saw that she was booked full with patients, including a follow-up with Mr. Anderson. Except for lunch, of course. Ha. "I'm not sure I can get away today," she hedged, not sure how Vale would feel about her having lunch with his cousin.

"Nonsense. Of course you can meet me for lunch." Sharon dismissed her objections in pure Wakefield expectation of the world bending to their will. "You're a brain doctor, so that means you're smart, right?"

"Uh, right," Faith said slowly, wondering where Sharon was going with her question.

"Steve had an affair," Sharon confessed, her tone going up several octaves. "Vale says I should just forget it, that the affair happened in the past, but I can't forget something like that, can I? Steve cheated on me. What's to say he wouldn't again? How can I ever trust him?"

Unbelievable. And yet another example of a marriage gone wrong. Another reason Faith should stay far away from men. Eventually they all ended up proving they were...well, men.

"I need someone really smart to talk to and Vale's who I usually go to, but he's all man on this subject. Plus, he's family. Please, Faith."

Feeling herself weaken, Faith took a deep breath. "Perhaps we could meet somewhere close to the office around noon?"

"Where have you been?" Vale demanded, shutting the door behind him with a loud thud as he entered Faith's office.

Wearing a boring gray suit and her glasses, she glanced up from the computer screen she was studying, eyed him as if he had no right to be in her personal space. As if she'd been on the computer for hours rather than only a few minutes. He knew that because he'd been listening for her return.

Should he remind her he owned the office? The whole building, for that matter?

"At lunch. Remember, that thing you insisted I take?" she pointed out with a sarcasm that didn't become her.

Fighting the wave of frustration he'd felt at Kay's news that Faith had called to say she was taking a long lunch, he placed his hands on his hips. "Insisting you take lunch did not entail your patients having to be rescheduled due to you deciding to take longer than the allotted time."

Caught off guard at his announcement, she blinked. Her mouth opened, then closed. "Since when did I start punching a time clock?" Her voice sounded as irritated as his.

"Who were you with, Faith?"

Because he couldn't stand not knowing. Not that it was any of his business, but Kay had led him to believe Faith had gone to lunch with a man. The man she'd been seeing prior to their weekend? A man she hadn't slept with up to that point, but what about now? Was she spreading those lush thighs and…? No, he wouldn't let his mind go there.

But, hell, if fire didn't burn in the pit of his stomach at the thought of another man touching her…

Regarding him with narrowed eyes, she unnecessarily adjusted her glasses. "Not that it's any of your business, but I had lunch with Sharon."

Sharon?

"What did she want?" Then it hit him. "She talked to you about Steve."

Faith nodded, a loose strand of her hair caressing her face as she did so. "About him cheating on her, yes."

Women. Steve loved Sharon with all his heart, was devastated at her reaction to his confession, yet Sharon now refused to speak to her new husband.

"It was a long time ago during a time when

they had broken up. She needs to quit acting like a spoiled child and go home to her husband."

"Excuse me?" Faith's brow arched upward. "During her *honeymoon*, she found out the man she loves cheated on her. I think she's entitled to be emotional right now."

"Sharon's being more than a little emotional. She's threatening to file for divorce," he said, knowing his cousin was acting rashly, rather than with logic. Steve loved her.

Faith just nodded and the way she didn't quite meet his eyes said she knew more than she was letting on.

"Don't tell me you encouraged her to continue with this nonsense?" When she didn't answer, Vale let out an exasperated sigh. "How dare you give her advice on marriage, or anything else? You know nothing of what our life is like. The media will be all over her and Steve. Everything either of them has ever done will be plastered in the gossip rags."

Faith placed her fingertip against the bridge of her glasses, thrust them up her pert nose. "It's not my place or yours to decide what's best for Sharon."

"She needs to stop this nonsense before she destroys her marriage. She needs to see reason."

Faith's eyes narrowed. "Reason being to take back a man who cheated on her?"

He placed both palms down on the deep-burgundy, high-back chair across from her desk, dug his fingers into the soft leather. "Don't pretend to be an expert in things you know nothing about."

"I know what she told me. Her husband cheated on her, destroyed her trust in him, and she wants a divorce."

"She acts as if he slept around after they were married. He didn't. They'd broken up at the time of his indiscretion."

Faith's mouth dropped open, then her eyes narrowed. "Isn't that just like a man, to focus on a technicality? If he loved her, whether or not they were having an off time shouldn't have mattered. According to Sharon, they broke up quite frequently, but always got back together.

She never slept with anyone else and feels he shouldn't have either."

Gritting his teeth, Vale squeezed the top of the chair. Was Faith purposely trying to antagonize him? Because of what had happened between them? "Steve didn't deserve her abandoning him in Rio during their honeymoon."

Faith's brow quirked. "Perhaps he should have thought about that prior to telling her during their *honeymoon* that he'd had sex with another woman, but no worries because she didn't mean anything to him and he and Sharon had broken up at the time so it didn't really count."

Vale wouldn't argue that Steve's timing had been lacking, but the man had thought he was doing the right thing, had wanted to clear his conscience, because he truly did love Sharon.

"I know my cousin. She's confused." He met Faith's gaze. "Don't you have enough problems with your own family's marital issues? Stay out of mine."

She sucked in air loudly, looked at him with shattered eyes, making him wish he could take back his words. But he couldn't and maybe he didn't even really want to.

Regardless, he'd had enough.

Faith stared at Vale's retreating back. Had he really just ordered her to stay out of his family's marital issues? Hadn't he been the one to drag her into his family's marital issues to begin with by insisting she be his "date" for his cousin's wedding to save him from his family's match-making?

Weeks of frustration at the change in their relationship, at his cold shoulder, rose to the surface, blowing her top like a champagne cork. Her anger spewed out in messy, foamy white bursts.

"Don't you order me around like you own me and then walk out of my office all sanctimonious and holier than thou," she retaliated, jumping up from her desk to chase after him.

Surprised by her outburst and probably more so by her gripping of his jacket and tugging him round to face her, Vale's gaze cut into her. She rushed on before he could stop her.

"If Sharon wants me as her friend, I'll see her any time she wants and there's nothing you can do about it."

"We're talking about *my* cousin," he reminded her, angry pink stains flushing his cheeks.

"Which doesn't mean you own her. Sharon is a grown woman and, yes, she may be confused right now, but that doesn't mean she needs some *man* telling her what she should and shouldn't be doing right now."

"Some man?" he growled. "Oh, you were just waiting to get that dig in, weren't you? This just reinforces all your hang-ups about relationships and marriage, doesn't it?"

"Marriage is an outdated sentiment. Disposable in today's society, just promises made that are only meant to be kept until the man grows bored and moves on. I want no part of it." Faith stood on tiptoe, nose to nose with him, hating that even in anger her body had taken notice of his proximity, of his spicy aftershave, of the sexuality radiating from his every pore.

"Obviously," he sneered. "But Sharon doesn't share that sentiment as she chose to marry Steve.

Keep yourself and your jaded views away from my family."

Did he have any idea that she wanted to pound her fists against his chest? Did he have any idea she'd cried over the loss of his friendship? Of all the precious moments they'd spent together? Of course not. Because if she wasn't willing to have sex with him, he obviously didn't want anything more to do with her.

"No, you, you *man*!" She wasn't sure if she was denying his request to stay away from his family or if she spat the word out in protest of him not caring at how they'd ruined their relationship, a relationship she'd treasured.

"This isn't up for debate." Angry sparks flew from his eyes and she was glad.

Anger meant she was eliciting some type of emotion from him. She wanted emotion, wanted a reaction from him. For weeks she'd been getting nothing but him ignoring her.

"You're right. It's not. You have no right to tell me what I can and cannot do," she insisted, earning herself a gritted-teeth growl from a man known for his cool composure.

Good. At this point she wanted a knock-down, drag-out fight. Arguing with him felt so much better than walking around on the eggshells she'd been treading since the morning after they'd come back from Cape May.

"Sure I do," he said arrogantly. "You work for me."

"Just because I work for you, it does not give you the right to say who I can and can't be friends with." Her chin rose another few notches.

"Then you'll be doing it elsewhere because as long as you work for me, you'll do what I say. Got it?"

Faith's stomach knotted, what was left of her heart shattered into dust, and pain like she'd never felt erupted deep within her, battling with her anger for pole position.

"Fine," she spat at him, clinging to her anger in the hope of abating her pain. "Consider this my official resignation. I quit. Effective immediately."

CHAPTER TEN

AT FAITH's threat, Vale's blood instantaneously froze to hard chunks of ice. Coldness seeped into his extremities, leaving him numb and spent.

"You can't quit," he told her, wanting to take her into his arms and shake her, but he didn't need to. Her entire body was already shaking, whether from anger or frustration or what he didn't know.

She crossed her arms over her chest, jutted her chin up at him, and gave him the most seething look he'd ever seen cross her face. "I just did."

"We have a contract," he reminded her, battling the frost claiming his insides, not liking the panic in his chest, knowing he couldn't let her quit. "One that says you work for me."

"Fine, take me to court," she said flippantly, not backing down from her position. "I'm sure any judge will release me under the circumstances."

"What circumstances?"

She rolled her eyes. "Oh, don't give me that. You know exactly what circumstances I'm referring to."

"Our sleeping together?"

She smiled, as pretty as you please. "What else?"

"You're being ridiculous, Faith. You can't quit because we slept together."

"No, you're the one who's ridiculous, Vale." His name came out a sarcastic slur. "Sleeping with you has apparently destroyed my career. Was I that bad in the sack?"

That bad? Shouldn't he be the one asking that question? He'd wanted to continue sleeping with her. She'd been the one to say no. "That's enough, Faith."

"No, it's not enough. Do you want to know what's enough? Me putting up with you ignoring me after what we shared. Me crying night after night, trying to figure out what I did wrong that weekend when the truth is I didn't do anything wrong. You did, you pompous jerk!"

He winced. He'd known she was hurting, that he'd hurt her by backing away from their friendship, but when he wanted her so badly, how could he spend time with her and not end up seducing her? She needed to realize that they were worth pursuing and not because he'd charmed his way between her delectable thighs.

His pride had come into play as well. He'd wanted her to admit she'd been wrong to push him away, that he'd been right to say he wanted to continue beyond their weekend together. Had he pushed her away for ever instead?

"I'm sorry if I hurt you."

"I don't want your pity or your apologies."

"What is it you want, Faith? I told you I still wanted you, that I wanted to explore what was happening between us. You were the one to say no. What would you have me do to make things right between us?"

She studied him for several seconds, then lowered her arms to her sides in a defeated gesture. "There's nothing you can do, Vale. It's too late."

He realized that now, realized that the moment he'd kissed her it had been too late to salvage their professional relationship.

Maybe he'd handled her rejection of him all wrong. But he hadn't been thinking clearly, still wasn't thinking clearly.

Faith was leaving him.

No, not him, she was leaving the clinic.

Hell, same difference. Either way, she would no longer be a part of his life.

If she refused to acknowledge that they'd had a chance for something special to develop between them, then maybe her leaving was for the best.

Maybe that was the only way for either of them to forget the weekend in Cape May.

"You win, Faith," he said in a low voice. "You're an excellent neurologist and the clinic will be taking a hard hit to lose you. Still, you can leave if that's what you want, but you know I don't want you to go. Not personally and not professionally."

He didn't want her to go. He wanted her to stay, to say they could pick up where they'd left off. But they'd just end up back at this same point.

Why delay the inevitable? Faith didn't want the same things he did.

"What you want is irrelevant to me, Vale. Totally irrelevant."

Had she still been screaming at him, he might have put her words down to emotional stress. But Faith wasn't screaming. She spoke with a calmness that chilled him. Almost as if she'd read his thoughts and was answering, assuring him that she didn't want him beyond the physical—and for once that wasn't enough.

"You don't mean that."

Surprise filled her eyes, and when she met his gaze, she shone with confidence. "Actually, I do. Goodbye, Vale. I'll send for my things."

"Faith." He grabbed her shoulder, refusing to let her pass, cursing himself for not being strong enough to let her go without one last desperate appeal for her to stay. "Don't go like this."

"Is there a better way for me to go? Some way you'd prefer? Maybe if I came into your office and told you I'd accepted an offer from another clinic so you wouldn't have to feel guilty over our liaison? Would that make you feel better? Would that free you from your guilt?"

He winced. Was that what the twinge in his chest was? Guilt? Guilt that he'd taken her virginity? Guilt that he couldn't look at her without wanting to strip her naked?

She was right. He did feel guilty. Guilt he clung to, because if what he was feeling wasn't guilt, then he'd have to find another label. Guilt was so much easier to deal with than the alternative.

"Do you have another offer, Faith? Is that what this is really about?"

First raking her gaze over him with cool disregard and a touch of disappointment, she nodded. "Yes, Vale, that's exactly what this is about. I'm leaving you for another clinic."

Blindly, chin high, shoulders straight, heart breaking, Faith made her way through the hallway leading away from her office, away from Vale. She kept her composure until the ladies' restroom door swung shut behind her.

Then sobs hit her in full force.

She shook. She ached. She sank against the inside of a stall and cried till her eyes throbbed.

What was wrong with her? She'd cried more in the past three weeks than she had her entire life. No man was worth this. Hadn't she watched her mother shed useless tears? Had she learned nothing at all from years of witnessing her mother's mistakes? From having lived through her father leaving?

"Faith?" a female voice asked from outside the stall. "Are you okay? What am I saying? Of course, you aren't okay. Can I come in? That is, well, maybe you could just come out of the stall instead?"

"Sharon?" Faith swiped at her eyes beneath her glasses, wishing she hadn't put on make-up that morning as she likely had raccoon eyes. "What are you doing here?"

"I heard your fight with Vale," the woman admitted, compassion filling her voice.

Great. Faith didn't need Sharon feeling sorry for her.

"I didn't mean to eavesdrop," she continued. "I thought of some things I'd forgotten to mention at lunch so I came back. I was outside your door, heard my name, and did exactly what I shouldn't have done. Eavesdropped."

Faith took a deep breath, hating that she hiccupped, hating that when she opened the stall door there was no way could she hide how pitifully she'd been crying. "I'm sorry you had to hear my argument with Vale."

"Why? You were wonderful."

Faith blinked, sure she'd misheard. She opened the stall to stare in shock through the tear-induced fog of her glasses at Vale's cousin. "I was?"

"Absolutely," Sharon replied. Reaching for a tissue and Faith's glasses, she took it upon herself to blot away Faith's tears. "I've never heard anyone put Vale in his place that way. Never. Even most of the family are a little scared of him." Sharon stepped back, surveyed her clean-up job of Faith's face, and smiled. "You and I are going to be great friends."

Faith's head was spinning. "But—"

"No buts." Sharon opened her purse, dug around until she pulled out a zippered pouch.

Removing liquid concealer, she squirted a pearl-size drop on her fingertip. "Look up," she ordered, dabbing beneath Faith's eyes, then smoothing out the make-up to her satisfaction. "Any woman who can stand up to my cousin and leave him speechless has my complete admiration."

The reality of what she'd done sank in. "Oh, God, I just quit my job."

"But you said you were going to a different clinic," Sharon pointed out, confusion marring her flawless complexion as she handed Faith a new tube of lipstick. "That's my favorite color, by the way. I always carry extras, just in case I lose one."

Vale's cousin carried extra tubes of the same shade of lipstick? Taking the lipstick, she read the label. Pouty Pink Passion.

"I lied," she admitted, peeling the plastic seal away and opening the tube to stare at the color. Not bad.

"Oh," Sharon said, her mouth forming a perfect circle and creases lining her forehead. "But you're still a brain doctor, right?"

Smoothing the lipstick onto her lips, rubbing her lips together to smooth out the cream, Faith nodded. "Yes, I'm still a neurologist. Just an unemployed one."

So why wasn't she freaking out? Why was she standing next to a bathroom stall, putting on make-up while chatting with Sharon Wakefield Woodard as if they were discussing the weather?

"Great!" Sharon clapped her hands in glee. "You'll work for yourself, start your own clinic, and be my doctor. Goodness knows, I need my head examined for getting married."

Faith's Pouty Passion Pink–covered lower lip dropped open. "I can't start my own clinic."

"Why not?" Sharon asked, so matter-of-factly that Faith stopped and asked herself the same question.

Why did she have to work for someone else? Let them decide her fate? Sure, prestige came with working for a clinic of Wakefield and Fishe's caliber, but prestige could be earned.

Then reality sank in again. "I appreciate your enthusiasm, but I don't have the money to start a clinic and get it off the ground."

"Hello..." Sharon rolled her eyes. "Yes, you do. I'm loaded and Vale is always telling me I need to make good investments, to find something to do with my life." She giggled with excitement. "I could work for you. Be your silent partner, even! This is the perfect solution for us both, Faith."

Stunned by Sharon's generosity and by her good humor when they were talking about Faith leaving her cousin's clinic, she shook her head. "I appreciate your offer, but I can't do that."

"Why not?"

"It wouldn't be ethical for me to accept money from my former employer's family."

"Ethics schmethics. We're talking about your future here and I'm offering you a way to really get under Vale's skin. The correct response is, 'Yes, ma'am, Miss Wakefield.'" Sharon held up her hand. "Don't even remind me that my legal last name is Woodard, because I want no part of Steve right now."

Faith stared at the crazy woman standing in the opening of the stall. "I don't want to get under Vale's skin."

"Yes," Vale's cousin assured her, looking way

too confident for a woman who had yo-yoed during their lunch between bawling her eyes out and professing that she wanted to castrate her soon-to-be ex-husband. "You do. Every woman wants to get under the skin of the man she loves." She gave a knowing smile. "Why else do you think I'm making Steve pay for his sins?"

Not quite believing her ears, Faith ventured a guess. "To get under Steve's skin?"

"Darned right." Sharon put her manicured hand on her hip and straightened her shoulders with determination. "He'll think twice before he ever cheats again."

Faith hadn't believed Vale when he'd commented on his family being crazy, had only believed they were the lovable, generous souls she'd met in Cape May. Now she knew he'd been on to something. Sharon was certifiable. Perhaps she herself was too, because a slow smile spread across her face and her future suddenly didn't look nearly so bleak.

Two weeks had passed since Faith had walked out of Vale's office. She wouldn't talk to him.

Not that Vale blamed her, but the entire situation grew more and more ridiculous. How had he ended up on Steve's side rather than his cousin's in an argument that shouldn't have been happening in the first place?

Sharon wouldn't return his calls. Faith wouldn't return his calls.

He rapped his knuckles against her apartment door yet again. Apparently, she wouldn't answer the door at her apartment either.

Unfortunately an angry little lady had opened her apartment door and threatened to call the police if he didn't leave.

"I need to talk to Faith," he explained, frustrated that he'd been the one pushed away, he'd been the one left behind, yet here he was at her apartment door and yet again she was ignoring him.

When a tiny dog launched past the woman and attached itself to his ankle, Vale was the one yelping in frustration and pain. The dog might be small but his teeth were sharp and sank into Vale's flesh with unerring ease.

"Don't hurt him," the woman squealed, coming

after the beast Vale was trying to shake free without permanently mangling his leg in the process.

"Don't hurt him?" Vale snorted, dancing around in effort to dislodge the dog. "What about me? This mutt is vicious."

"Yoda, get back here," the older woman called to the dog Vale had managed to free from his flesh but which was still latched on to his pants with tenacious determination.

Then what the woman had said sank in as surely as the dog's teeth had.

"Yoda?" He glanced behind her. Sure enough. Apartment 907. The angry lady was Faith's dog-sitter. "This is Faith's dog."

Vale smiled a devilish smile, knowing he wouldn't have to worry about whether or not Faith took his calls or answered the door. She'd be calling him before the day ended.

Bending down, he scooped the dog into his arms, prepared for the pain that was sure to come in doing so. He wasn't disappointed.

Sometimes getting what you wanted was a

pain in the kisser. Or, as in this case, a pain in the arm.

He turned to the dog-sitter who scowled at him and was telling Yoda to "get him".

"Tell Faith I have her dog. If she wants Yoda back, she knows where to find him."

Faith blinked at her neighbor. "He did what?"

When Mrs. Beasley had burst into the tiny office space she'd rented, face red, chest puffing, eyes wild, Faith had feared for the elderly woman's life.

"That handsome devil who you went away with, the one you've been moping around over, he dognapped Yoda!" Mrs. Beasley panted, her wrinkled hands fluttering against her heaving chest. "Call the police, now, so they can catch the scoundrel."

"Sit down, Mrs. Beasley." Sharon came over to the older woman, handed her a glass of water, and motioned to the empty chair she'd placed behind the exhausted woman. "You're going to have a stroke if you don't calm down."

"I'm not going to have a stroke," the woman

denied, her face flushed with excitement. "We have to do something. That awful man has stolen Faith's dog."

"Hmm, he always did want a dog, but taking yours is a bit much, even for a Wakefield," Sharon mused from beside Faith, both of them eyeing Mrs. Beasley with concern.

The poor woman really had been frantic when she'd burst into Faith's new office a couple of blocks over from their apartment complex.

"Do you think we should call for an ambulance? You're looking a little winded, Mrs. B."

"An ambulance?" Mrs. Beasley stared at her as if she was daft. "We need the SWAT team, not a defibrillator."

"It's okay," Faith assured her neighbor, taking her pulse and respirations. Tachypneic and tachycardic. She patted her neighbor's shaky hand, motioned for Sharon to get her a blood-pressure cuff and stethoscope. "Vale won't hurt Yoda."

At least, Faith didn't think he would.

"He might," Mrs. Beasley cried. "Yoda could tell he was a rascally fellow and didn't like him one bit. Even if he was dashing."

Wasn't it just like Vale to have caught Mrs. Beasley's eye even while the woman had been threatening to have him thrown into jail?

"What did Yoda do?" Faith took her blood pressure. Slightly elevated at 140/90, but not too bad considering how upset the woman was.

"Attacked him."

Mouth agape, Faith asked, "Yoda attacked Vale?"

Mrs. Beasley nodded proudly. "Probably brought blood with the way he was attached to his leg. That'll teach him to keep banging on your door and disturbing the peace."

Vale had been banging on her apartment door?

Faith bit the inside of her lip.

Maybe she should have answered one of his zillion calls to her cellphone, but she hadn't. She'd erased his messages without listening to them. Talking to him would accomplish nothing. Not at this point. Maybe when time had passed and she was stronger, when he didn't make her dream of things she knew better than to dream about. But not yet because her dreams were filled with him.

"That's why Vale dognapped Yoda?" She tried to wrap her brain around how Vale had gone from beating on her apartment door to stealing her dog. "Because Yoda attacked him?"

"I've no idea why the scoundrel took Yoda." Mrs. Beasley shuddered at what she obviously considered a harrowing experience. "He didn't ask for a ransom, just said if you wanted your dog back, you knew where to find him."

Faith fell back into a chair, her hand going to her temple.

Yoda dognapped by her former boss.

If she wanted her baby back, she had to go to him.

She had a good mind to do as Mrs. Beasley suggested and call the police and have Vale arrested. Watching his arrogant face plastered across the nine o'clock news would please her to no end. The great Dr. Vale Wakefield, talented neurosurgeon and playboy heir to a real estate empire, arrested for stealing a *helpless* dog. Oh, the press would have a field day.

But instead of picking up her phone, she glanced at a giggling Sharon.

"This really isn't funny, you know," she advised the woman who was quickly becoming a dear friend. "Your cousin has my dog."

"You have to give him points for creativity. Dognapping Yoda was quite ingenious in assuring you'd stop avoiding him." Sharon smiled smugly. "We Wakefields are known for our resourcefulness when it comes to getting what we want."

"You could go and get Yoda for me," Faith suggested, knowing Sharon's answer even before the woman said a word. Despite not being willing to budge an inch where Steve was concerned, Sharon seemed quite positive Faith should give Vale a chance to prove that he really had wanted to continue their relationship, that he'd wanted more than just a weekend fling with her, that she really was different from all the women he'd known.

But why give him a chance to prove that when doing so would only lead to pain down the road? Horrible pain because he wouldn't stick around and then where would she be?

"No way." Sharon shook her head. "Yoda is

your dog. You know he has no taste and gnaws at my shoes. If you want the mangy mutt back, you'll have to go and get him. Personally, I say good riddance."

But the amused gleam in Sharon's eyes told she was teasing. Mostly. Yoda had yet to be completely forgiven for destroying an Italian shoe he'd mistaken for an expensive chew toy.

Vale wanted to talk to her. They'd talk. But she didn't have anything different to tell him from what she'd said two weeks ago. Not really.

Of course there were all the things she hadn't said that last day. Like how much she missed the time they'd spent together. How much she missed consulting with him, laughing with him, just being with him. How much she missed how it had felt to lie in his arms and breathe in his masculine scent.

No, she hadn't told him any of those things and being away from the office for two weeks hadn't helped matters, had perhaps made things worse.

She missed Vale. Horribly. With all her heart.

Wherein lay the problem.

The truth was that Vale had stolen much more than her dog.

And as much as she'd like to think staying away from him would help prevent her from hurting, she wasn't so sure anything could help her from the devastation of being without Vale. Which made her no better than her mother. Destined to move through life searching for an elusive feeling she'd known once and desperately strove to find again.

"Fine," she told the two women anxiously waiting to hear her plans. "I'll go and get my dog."

CHAPTER ELEVEN

FAITH hadn't been inside Wakefield and Fishe since the day she'd quit her dream job. Marcus Fishe had come to her, tried to get her to tell him what had happened, had probably already figured out the truth.

In the end, Vale's partner said he hated to lose her, that the clinic would provide a generous severance package, see to it all her patients were taken care of with minimal disruption, and that he understood her need to move on. He hadn't really, though. No one in the neurology profession would.

Wakefield and Fishe was *the* place to work.

Faith greeted the Wakefield Tower night security guard, who smiled and had obviously been told to expect her as he waved her in, no questions asked even though he had to know she no longer worked in the building.

Vale was here. Waiting on her. Forcing her to talk to him.

What was left to say? She'd already said more than she probably should have on the day she'd lost her temper and quit.

Apparently, he hadn't said all he'd wanted to say. To get her dog back, she'd listen to whatever he needed to get off his chest.

But, really, what was the point? He should be grateful she'd walked away rather than stick around mooning over him, because she'd had enough of him ignoring her just because she'd said no to continuing their affair.

When she stepped onto the fifty-sixth floor, her breath caught as she took in the scope of Wakefield and Fishe's reception area. She'd loved working here, loved working with Vale.

But that was in the past, and this wasn't a time for recriminations. She'd moved beyond that, was putting the pieces of her life back together, with Sharon's friendship and silent financial partnership in planning for her own neurology clinic.

She didn't need a man in her life.

The office was unusually quiet for only a little after 8:00 p.m. Had Vale sent everyone home at a decent hour for once?

Part of her wanted to go to her office, to see what had happened to the room she'd happily occupied for a year and a half of her life. The best year and a half of her life? But she wasn't here for reminiscing either. She was here for her dog. Nothing else.

Forcing one high-heeled foot in front of the other (Sharon had insisted she deck herself out), she made a beeline for Vale's office and didn't bother knocking. He knew she was there. The security guard would have alerted him the moment she stepped into the elevator.

He sat at his desk, pretending to read a document. She knew he was pretending, didn't know why he bothered.

He looked wonderful, a sight for sore eyes. Why did just seeing him undo what little progress she'd made over the past two weeks on putting him behind her?

Who was she kidding? She hadn't made any

progress on getting over Vale. Perhaps she never would.

His gaze lifted to hers, studied her with his intense blue eyes. "You came."

Had he for one moment thought she wouldn't?

"You have my dog. I want him back." She used a tone of voice she hoped warned she wasn't to be messed with.

His gaze flickered to his desk, lingered a moment on nothing in particular, before meeting hers again. "Sit down, Faith."

Why was he torturing them this way? She'd stepped out of the picture and planned to stay out of the picture. He should be thanking his lucky stars she hadn't made a stink about the Cape May weekend.

Yet he didn't look as if he felt lucky.

He looked as if he was nervous. Which was insane. Vale didn't scare easily, if at all.

Yet, he did look nervous. From the way his gaze darted around to the way he fidgeted with the papers on his desk.

What was she doing? Looking for excuses for

Vale's behavior? There were no excuses for how they'd ruined their relationship.

"This isn't a social visit, Vale. Give me my dog."

He stood up, towering above her and making her believe she'd imagined whatever vulnerability she'd thought she'd seen in him. He wasn't vulnerable. He was a Wakefield. One who didn't care who he hurt, just so long as he got what he wanted.

And for whatever reason, he'd thought he wanted to continue their affair and she'd thwarted his plans. That had to be what this was about.

"Not until you listen to me."

Faith plopped down in the chair in front of his desk, crossing her legs and staring at him as if he were a bug under a microscope. "Fine." She attempted to sound bored. "Get to talking because I've a lot of things to do. Places to go, people to see, you know the routine."

Vale raked his gaze over Faith. She was wearing make-up, no glasses, and was dressed in feminine clothes that accented the body he craved.

Her hair was down, brushing over her shoulders, teasing him with its multifaceted golden colors, teasing him with memories of his fingers clenched in the soft strands when he'd made love to her.

He'd never seen anyone more beautiful.

But, truthfully, what she was wearing didn't matter. Just that she was there.

"I've missed you."

"Having trouble finding someone else to handle your calls?" she snipped, picking an invisible speck off her short skirt.

Had she purposely worn the skirt to distract him with those long legs of hers? Had she known he'd take one look and start remembering what having those legs wrapped around his waist felt like?

He moved around his desk, sat on the corner, staring at her. "You didn't quit because of fielding calls on mutual patients."

She didn't answer, just examined her fingernails. When she looked up, their gazes met.

Enough was enough. If they were going to get anywhere one of them had to take a leap into uncharted waters. He'd never considered himself to be a coward, but he'd prefer her to go first, to admit that she missed him, missed not only their previous relationship but also the closeness they'd developed during Sharon's wedding weekend.

Not that he expected her to. Not after what he'd done.

He'd hurt her with his high-handedness.

As much as he hated it, he'd have to grovel if he wanted her forgiveness.

"I'm sorry for what happened the day you quit."

Her gaze snapped to his, but otherwise she just sat, long legs crossed, not saying a word. But her fingernails curled into her palms. She wasn't as immune to what he was saying as she acted.

"I was wrong to ask you to stay away from Sharon. I wasn't thinking clearly and hadn't been for a few weeks."

"Agreed." Again, she went for bored, but those fingers remained dug into her palms. "Can I go now?"

"No, you can't go." He stood up, unable to

remain perched on the edge of the desk. "I don't want you to ever go, Faith. I want you back."

She jumped to her feet, her heels putting her at mere inches beneath his eye level. "You can't have me back."

Her eyes glittered almost violently. Her hands had fisted at her sides. Her chin had lifted in the most stubborn of tilts. He'd never wanted her more.

"I refuse to accept that as your final answer. I will have you back, Faith. One way or another, you will be mine again."

"My final answer?" Her mouth dropped open and she shook her head at him. "This isn't some game where you get to toy with me until I change my mind. I'm not coming back to the clinic. Or any clinic. I'm opening my own practice."

The pride in her voice raised his admiration for her. Faith was a survivor, a woman who could make her own way in the world. No surprise there. He'd always recognized that she was a rare jewel. Had instantly recognized that he wanted her on his side. He just hadn't meant to come to depend upon her quite so much. To the point that he truly had wanted her at his side on each and every patient consult. At his side all the time.

"If you won't come back to me, I'll come to you, Faith."

"What?" she asked, clearly confused. No wonder. He himself certainly wouldn't have understood fifteen seconds before.

"Hire me," he urged, knowing exactly what he had to do, what he was willing to do to have Faith back in his life. "I have excellent references, am willing to work cheap, and haven't lost my clinical skills." He hesitated, took a strand of her hair between his fingers, wanting to take hold of so much more. "Actually, the only thing I've lost that's ever mattered to me is you."

"Is that the problem, Vale? I walked out on you?" She pulled free of his touch, just as he'd known she would. "Let me remind you of how things really went down. You pushed me so far away I had no choice but to walk. For three weeks you ignored that I even existed, treating me like I didn't exist. Maybe I'd been spoiled by you including me in so many of your cases, but to suddenly be cut out for no reason other than that I refused to continue to have sex with you was wrong."

She was right, but how could he explain the way he'd felt when he'd looked into her eyes in the lighthouse and known the weekend wasn't nearly enough time with her? The way he'd felt when she'd told him she didn't want to continue their relationship?

"I couldn't be near you without wanting you, Faith."

She shoved against his chest, her hands sending shock waves through him. "You were around me for months and months without wanting me. You just want what you think you can't have," she continued, practically in his face. "Typical man."

"Don't fool yourself into believing that I can't have you if I wanted you, Faith," he warned, pride kicking in. "We both know that if I touched you right now you'd go up in flames."

"You're wrong." But she was lying. "You're a player who couldn't hold on to his new toy quite as long as he'd have liked. We both know if we'd pursued this you would have grown bored before long."

Vale shifted his jaw, reminding himself not to lose his temper, wondering why she was the only person able to push him beyond the point of reason. "I never made you promises or told you I was some great catch, but I was sincere when I told you I wanted us to continue what we'd started."

"Your point is?" She quirked her brow at him, obviously having already lost her temper. "Shall I remind you that I left? That I understood you never made me any promises?"

"I don't need reminding, Faith. I know you left me." For two weeks he'd been able to think of little else. Faith had left him. He missed her. He wanted her back. Whatever the cost. "Shall I remind you that I'm the one fighting to have you back in my life?"

She stared blankly at him.

"I'm serious about the job, Faith. Sharon did tell me your plans, so perhaps you no longer want to work here." He shrugged. "If you won't come back to Wakefield and Fishe, I'll come to work for you."

She studied him with suspicious green eyes. "Why would you want to do that?"

"Have you not listened to anything I've said? I miss you. I want you in my life. If not as my lover, then as my friend, my co-worker. Whatever you're willing to give me, I'll take."

She closed her eyes, swallowed. "Why are you doing this to me, Vale? I was here for eighteen months and you never noticed me. Why now, when I'm moving on, putting the pieces of my life together in a way I believe I can be happy about? Just leave me alone, please. I don't want to be hurt by you and we both know we'd never work out in the long run."

With her eyes squeezed shut, she looked so vulnerable. Part of him wanted to just step away, to let her be. But the truth was he *had* noticed her. Maybe he hadn't realized just how much he'd noticed her, how much he'd come to expect to spend his days with her, but he had noticed her.

Maybe he hadn't been willing to admit just

how much he'd expected her to be a part of his life because then he would have had to examine why that was so.

The thought of losing her though had him examining all kinds of things he'd prefer not to.

"I can't leave you alone, Faith," he answered honestly, causing her eyes to flutter open.

"Why not?"

"Because I'm not me when you're not here."

Her gaze lifted to his. "Explain."

If only he could. "Nothing works the same when you're not with me. I don't work the same. It's like I get up on the wrong side of the bed and my days go downhill from there."

Her forehead wrinkled. "What are you saying? That I'm your lucky mojo or something?"

He shook his head. "It isn't that."

"Then what is it?" she demanded, losing patience with him again. "Tell me why I'm here, Vale. Why you dognapped my defenseless dog."

Defenseless, his hind end.

"I need you here, Faith. I need you with me."

"I thought you were willing to come to work for my clinic," she countered.

"Is that an offer?"

"No." But he saw the wall she'd built around her crack, knew he was starting to get through to her, and that made him all the more determined to lay everything on the line, to make her see reason.

"I think about you all the time," he admitted, chipping away at the crack, wanting to completely tear down the wall she'd built around herself. "When I wake up, when I go to sleep, all in between. I think about you."

She took a step back, bumping against his desk. "Guilt does strange things to a person's conscience."

"It's not guilt I feel for you, Faith."

As if she couldn't stand, she sat on the edge of his desk. "What do you feel?"

"This." He took her hand into his and kissed each fingertip. "This is what I feel, Faith."

She trembled. "That's just sex."

He shook his head. "I can get sex from anyone, Faith. I don't need sex, but I do need you. *You.*"

Her lip disappeared between her teeth. "You need me?"

"As much as the air I breathe. Quit shutting me out of your life."

She winced, pulled her hand free from his and slid her fingers beneath her thigh protectively. "This makes no sense, Vale. I was here every day, wanting us to go back to the way we were before we went to Cape May, and you shut me out. It was you who pushed me away. You can't go changing your mind."

"Why not?" he asked, cupping her face. "Why can't I admit I made a miscalculation and pushed away the best thing that's ever happened to me?"

"Because…because…" Her eyes closed again. "You just can't."

"People make mistakes, Faith. I thought if I stayed away you'd realize we were worth giving a chance. I thought you'd miss me and come to me. You didn't, and the longer you stayed away the more frustrated I got. I took that frustration out on you. Forgive me."

Moisture welled in her eyes, but she held fast, shaking her head. "I can't."

"Why not?"

"Because you'll hurt me again, and I don't think I could bear it when you did."

"Give me a chance to prove I won't."

She shook her head. "There's nothing you can do because I know you'll hurt me. You're you and I'm me and even under the best of circumstances couples don't last. We don't stand a chance."

He sighed. "I never meant to hurt you. You must know that. You shut me out too, Faith. I was offering you something I'd never offered any woman, was wanting things with you I'd never wanted before. You weren't the only one hurting. You're not being rational."

She crossed her arms across her chest, glared at him. "Nowhere is there a law written that says I have to be rational."

"Fine, then be irrational and marry me."

Faith's eyes bugged out of her head.

His probably did too.

Where had his proposal come from? He hadn't intended to ask Faith to marry him. He wanted her back in his life, but marriage? That was extreme.

But even as he thought it, if marrying Faith meant having her back in his life, proving to her he wanted her in his life long-term, he'd walk down the aisle. He enjoyed her company. She was smart, beautiful, and he craved her body.

"No."

He gritted his teeth, staring at her in disbelief. "No?"

"No, I won't marry you. You know how I feel about marriage. Do I need to spell it out for you?"

"Apparently," he said dryly.

"I don't need you or any man in my life."

Enough was enough. He'd tired of the games, of the going back and forth. "We both know you're in love with me, Faith. Quit clinging to your hang-ups about marriage because of your father leaving, because of your mother's multiple weddings."

Her eyes narrowed and her mouth dropped open in disbelief. "I've never told you that I loved you."

"Haven't you?" He called her bluff.

"I'd definitely recall if I'd said 'I love you' to any man. I haven't. Ever."

He leaned in, placed his hands to either side of her on his desk, trapping her beneath his gaze. "You don't love me?"

Not meeting his eyes, she swallowed. "I—I… well…"

"Well, what?" He wasn't going to let her off the hook. Not until she answered him. "It's a yes or no question. Either you do or you don't."

She took a deep breath. "The point isn't whether or not I love you."

"Then you do love me?" His pulse hammered at his throat, beating him into a dizzy head spin as he waited for her to answer. Why was hearing her say the words so important?

"Quit twisting my words."

"Quit being stubborn, and admit you've missed me as much as I've missed you."

"Fine, I've missed you, but that changes nothing."

Vale smiled. Finally he was making progress, was stepping behind that wall. "And you've thought about me?"

"I've thought about you." Her chin lifted. "Occasionally."

"In the mornings?" he pressed. "In the evenings? In the shower?"

"Vale, this is crazy," she scolded, frowning, twisting free of where he had her pinned on his desk. She walked across his office, standing beside the long mahogany work table they'd spent many a night sitting at with data files spread out around them. "I'm pleading the Fifth."

"Those who plead the Fifth are always guilty, Faith." He stood, moved to just behind her, tempted to touch, but waited for a sign she'd welcome him.

"That's not true," she denied, her gaze narrowed.

"Sure it is."

"Then answer me this—why do you want to marry me?"

"I'm not pleading the Fifth, if that's what you're expecting."

"But you aren't answering, are you?" she challenged, looking so sure of herself Vale had to slide his hands into his pocket to keep from

taking her into his arms and kissing her stubborn mouth.

"I want to marry you so I can hold you in my
arms every single night."

Her eyes widened.

"I want to marry you so I can wake up and see
you first thing every single morning."

Her lips parted.

"I want to marry you so I can push up your
skirt and make love to you any time I want,
starting right now on the table you're leaning
against."

"Oh." She straightened from the table.

"I want to marry you so I can kiss away your
tears and take you with me to family functions
so you can protect me from my crazy family."

Her fingers clenched and unclenched at her
sides.

"But mostly, Faith, I want to marry you so I
don't ever have to be without you again. I want
you to be mine."

CHAPTER TWELVE

FAITH stood stock still, uncertain what to say or do.

Vale wanted to marry her?

What rabbit hole had she fallen into and bumped her head? Then the obvious reason for his pursuit hit her.

Why hadn't she realized? She should have already told him, should have realized that was why he'd kept calling.

"I'm not pregnant if you're concerned that something resulted from our weekend."

Surprise filled his eyes. "I didn't think you were, Faith, but we can rectify that if you'd like to be."

This time Faith was the one filled with surprise. Was he kidding?

"Quit saying things like that!" Didn't he realize that his words were like a searing iron to her heart? Words that a deeply buried part of her wanted to believe yet couldn't.

"Why?"

"Because you don't mean them."

His face clouded. "You don't think I'd strip you naked and make love to you right here, right now, on the table behind you in the hope of making you pregnant?"

Had someone drugged him? Or maybe he'd fallen into a rabbit hole and hit his head. Because, one way or another, one of them was out of their head.

"I've repeatedly told you I'm sorry, Faith. Is it so impossible to forgive me? To trust me?"

"Yes!"

"Why?"

"Because if I forgive you, if I trust you, then I have no reason to stay away from you." Her eyes widened and her hand popped over her mouth simultaneously at her admission.

"Would that be so bad?" he asked gently, taking her fingers into his and pulling her hand away from her mouth.

She closed her eyes. "Yes."

"Why?"

"Quit asking me why!"

"Then I'll ask you to love me, Faith, because I want your love every day for the rest of our lives."

She blinked. "Since when?"

"Since you walked out on me and took my heart with you."

Her face squished into contorted confusion. "What are you saying?"

He smiled down at her. "What I've been trying to say since you walked into this room."

Faith's heart tapped a wild beat in her chest. Could it be true? Could he be telling her what she thought he was telling her? Could this really be happening? Did she want this to be happening?

And if it was, could she take a chance on Vale? Could she believe he could really love her? Could really want to spend his life with her and wouldn't leave her? Oh, God, what if he left?

But what if he didn't ever leave?

What if he really did love her and wanted to

be with her for ever? Wouldn't that be worth any risk?

"Tell me," she whispered, staring into his eyes and seeing everything she couldn't quite believe reflected in the way he was looking at her.

"I love you, Faith." He cupped her face, brushing his thumb along her jaw line. "With all my heart and all my soul and all that I am, I love you, and I want to spend the rest of my life giving my love to you. Open up and let me."

She hadn't dreamed it was possible. Hadn't even contemplated what he was saying as a realistic possibility.

But Vale didn't hide his emotions, didn't attempt to mask them. He let his feelings for her shine in his eyes and she basked in the glory, letting his love thaw the wall she'd protected her heart behind since the day her father had walked out, since the first time she'd watched her mother walk down the aisle.

"This is crazy," Vale muttered, and took her in his arms before she could say anything. "If you won't let me tell you, if you won't believe my words, I'm going to show you."

With an offer like that on the table, Faith held her tongue. But when his lips covered hers, she kissed him back with the desperation of a woman who'd thought she'd forever lost the man she loved. With the joy of a woman who'd found him again.

Loved. Oh, God. She loved Vale.

With all her heart and all her being. Which left her so vulnerable. But if he was just as vulnerable to her, if he was there to look out for her vulnerable heart and vice versa, everything would be okay, right?

Oh! She couldn't think about that right now. Not when Vale's hands were everywhere. Cupping her face, tangled in her hair, beneath her blouse.

She didn't stop him when he made haste of ridding her of her clothes. Didn't stop him when he laid her back naked on the table while he shed his suit in record speed.

She certainly didn't stop him when he spread her legs and thrust inside her. She clung to his shoulders, clung to his body, loving him with all her heart and all her body.

Deeper and deeper he surged inside her, taking her back to that magical place she'd called Cape May but which had really been in his arms. Taking her back to explosive ecstasy.

Her thighs spasmed in sweet, hot throbs, pulsing in rhythm with her heartbeat. With his heartbeat.

Their heartbeat.

"I love you," she mouthed on the peak of her orgasm, feeling his body tighten against hers, feeling him lose his control and explode deep inside her.

Body slick with sweat, he rested his forehead against hers and stared into her eyes. "You'll marry me?"

She bit the inside of her lower lip. "Marriage scares me."

"I won't settle for less, Faith. I want the world to know you're mine."

"And that you're mine?"

"I am yours, Faith. Completely and irrevocably. I'll never leave you. Trust me."

Heart slamming against her ribcage, she wrapped her arms around his neck, holding him close. "It's not as if I really have a choice, is it? Now that you've made up your mind you want to marry me, you won't stop till I say yes."

"We Wakefields always get what we want."

She smiled up at him, awe still filling her at the magic this man had brought into her life. "You do realize that if we marry, I'll be a Wakefield, too?"

He looked at her with pure unadulterated love reflecting in his eyes. "And what is it you want, Faith? Because I'll give you anything within my power."

"You."

"You have me. Always and for ever."

They dressed slowly—so slowly they ended up undressed again rather than clothed.

This time Vale made love to her more slowly, gently, staring into her eyes with each thrust of his body into hers. Deeper and deeper until he was so tangled with her she didn't know where she ended and he began.

Her breaths came in ragged pants. Her heart

beat thudded in arrhythmic bursts. Her soul merged with his.

When he came, she cried out his name, cradling him in her body, stunned by what they'd shared.

Stunned by how loved she felt.

Stunned by how much she trusted him.

Stunned by the fact they'd made love twice without protection.

"Vale?"

"Hmm?"

"I do love you and I will marry you, but I'm not ready for a baby."

He rose up on his elbow, staring down at her. "No? I'm in no rush to start a family. The idea of having you to myself for a while appeals." He waggled his brows knowingly. "But when you're ready to start trying for a baby, I'll be an eager participant." His lips quirked into a half-smile. "What are you ready for, Faith?"

"You did offer me my job back," she reminded him, sitting up and reaching for her clothes.

He watched her replace her bra, fastening the

hooks between her breasts. "I also offered to come to work for you."

"I doubt starting a new business and getting married at the same time would be a wise decision." She pulled her blouse over her head, straightening the material at her waist, and looked around the table for her panties. Looking way too sexy, he held up her panties like a prized trophy. Faith rolled her eyes and snatched her silky underwear from him. "I loved working here with you, our research and the progress we're making on Parkinson's."

He sat up, pulled on his boxer briefs and slacks. Not bothering with his shirt, he leaned against the table. She tucked her blouse into her skirt. He stood silent a few minutes, then shifted his gaze to her.

"If starting your own clinic is what you want, we'll make it happen, do our research there." He sucked in a deep breath, met her gaze. "I don't want us being together to stand in the way of your dreams. Not ever."

Straightening from slipping her shoes back onto her feet so he wouldn't tower over her, she turned to him. Vale was a top-notch neurosurgeon, used to having his way, leading the pack. Was he seriously saying he'd help her build a neurology practice of her own?

"You'd really come work for me if I wanted my own clinic?"

He nodded. "In a heartbeat."

She stared at him in wonder, seeing the sincerity shining in his eyes. "I believe you would."

One corner of his mouth lifted and he gave a low laugh. "Haven't you figured out the truth yet, Faith? I'd move the world if that's what it took to make you happy, to make you mine for ever."

"No moving the world necessary." Pressing her palms to his bare chest, she smiled up at him, happier than she could recall ever being. "But I would like my dog back."

He grinned. "About that…"

Faith narrowed her gaze, giving him a playful glare. "What have you done to my poor Yoda?"

He held up his arm, displaying the tiny teeth marks. "Your poor Yoda is anything but poor. We need to work on his people skills."

Faith rubbed her finger over the red spots. "He was just trying to defend my honor."

"We need to sit down and have a talk with him, let him know that in the future that's my job."

"Where is Yoda?"

"At Sharon's."

"Sharon's?" Faith shook her head in wry amusement. Her friend had sure played it cool that evening. Faith had never suspected a thing. "She was in on this? Agreed to watch Yoda?"

He shook his head. "Nope, but I shut the little *Cujo* into her bedroom along with water, food, and newspaper. I figure he should be okay there for a few hours until she comes home and finds him."

Uh-oh. Faith grimaced. "You didn't happen to notice if her closet door was shut, did you?"

Looking confused, Vale shrugged. "I didn't notice. Why?"

Faith started laughing. "You are going to be in so much trouble when she discovers Yoda. Sharon isn't Yoda's biggest fan."

"See…" he grinned "…another example of needing to work on your dog's people skills."

"Maybe it's just Wakefields he takes issue with."

"That may present a problem in the near future, then."

She smiled up at him, loving the way he looked at her, at the warmth in his eyes. "Why's that?"

He lifted her chin, kissed her. "Because just as soon as it can be arranged you're going to be my wife, making you a Wakefield, too."

EPILOGUE

THE sun was shining on the first day of August. A gentle breeze blew in off the Atlantic and butterflies fluttered around the grounds of the Cape May lighthouse.

When Vale had first suggested having their wedding at the lighthouse, she'd thought he was teasing. When she'd realized he wasn't, she'd agreed that the lighthouse was the perfect place to start the rest of their lives.

Unlike his cousin's wedding, they'd opted for small, and had somehow managed to keep their upcoming nuptials out of the press.

Faith had invited her mother and stepfather, a beaming Mrs. Beasley, and a couple of friends from med school and work. Vale had his mother, Sharon, Angela, their parents, and Marcus Fishe, who served as his best man. Sharon stood next to Faith as her matron of honor.

Vale had also invited Steve, but mostly so the handsome footballer's presence could get under Sharon's skin.

All Wakefields apparently enjoyed getting under people's skins and based on how the former beauty queen kept stealing glances at her estranged husband her skin was crawling.

Vale had wanted to marry at the top of the lighthouse, but had conceded that Faith would have problems with the one hundred and ninety-nine steps in her wedding gown.

He'd offered to carry her, but thoughts of him being too tired for their wedding night had Faith convincing him that standing just behind the lighthouse on the grassy fenced lawn would be perfect, and a lot less windy for their photos.

Faith had struggled with asking stepfather number six to walk her down the aisle and had ended up deciding to walk alone. Her mother had seemed to understand. Vale, however, had wanted to track down her real father, to help her put to rest her abandonment issues. She'd assured him that he'd already done that by loving her. She didn't need anything more to have her happily-ever-after.

When the wedding march began to play, Faith walked to the man she loved with all her heart. The stubborn man who had so much pride and arrogance, but also the capacity to love her fully, completely, and without holding anything back.

The man who gave her so much. The whole world.

He was her whole world.

She handed her simple bouquet of wildflowers to Sharon, then turned to face the man she'd spend the rest of her life loving and being loved by.

The only other member of the wedding party was a tiny cream-colored poodle with a tiny black bowtie collar.

Yoda followed Faith down the aisle, sat at her feet, and quirked his head in silence at the vows being exchanged.

"I do," Faith promised, not able to keep the tears of joy from her eyes as she slid the ring onto the third finger of Vale's left hand.

When he took her hand in his, stared deeply

into her eyes, his love shining as brightly as the sun above them, happy bubbles danced in her belly.

"I do," he promised, placing the golden band symbolizing that promise on Faith's finger. "For ever and always, I do."

Her insides melted and her knees wobbled.

"You may now kiss your bride," the minister told Vale.

His hands caressed her neck, holding her as if she were a fragile flower. "I love you, Mrs. Wakefield."

Then he kissed her, sealing his promise for all time.

Faith returned his kiss, knowing deep in her heart that, although there would be times of troubled waters just as there were in any relationship, their love would light the course safely back to each other.

* * * * *

Mills & Boon® Large Print
Medical

January

THE PLAYBOY OF HARLEY STREET	Anne Fraser
DOCTOR ON THE RED CARPET	Anne Fraser
JUST ONE LAST NIGHT…	Amy Andrews
SUDDENLY SINGLE SOPHIE	Leonie Knight
THE DOCTOR & THE RUNAWAY HEIRESS	Marion Lennox
THE SURGEON SHE NEVER FORGOT	Melanie Milburne

February

CAREER GIRL IN THE COUNTRY	Fiona Lowe
THE DOCTOR'S REASON TO STAY	Dianne Drake
WEDDING ON THE BABY WARD	Lucy Clark
SPECIAL CARE BABY MIRACLE	Lucy Clark
THE TORTURED REBEL	Alison Roberts
DATING DR DELICIOUS	Laura Iding

March

CORT MASON – DR DELECTABLE	Carol Marinelli
SURVIVAL GUIDE TO DATING YOUR BOSS	Fiona McArthur
RETURN OF THE MAVERICK	Sue MacKay
IT STARTED WITH A PREGNANCY	Scarlet Wilson
ITALIAN DOCTOR, NO STRINGS ATTACHED	Kate Hardy
MIRACLE TIMES TWO	Josie Metcalfe

April

BREAKING HER NO-DATES RULE	Emily Forbes
WAKING UP WITH DR OFF-LIMITS	Amy Andrews
TEMPTED BY DR DAISY	Caroline Anderson
THE FIANCÉE HE CAN'T FORGET	Caroline Anderson
A COTSWOLD CHRISTMAS BRIDE	Joanna Neil
ALL SHE WANTS FOR CHRISTMAS	Annie Claydon

May

THE CHILD WHO RESCUED CHRISTMAS	Jessica Matthews
FIREFIGHTER WITH A FROZEN HEART	Dianne Drake
MISTLETOE, MIDWIFE...MIRACLE BABY	Anne Fraser
HOW TO SAVE A MARRIAGE IN A MILLION	Leonie Knight
SWALLOWBROOK'S WINTER BRIDE	Abigail Gordon
DYNAMITE DOC OR CHRISTMAS DAD?	Marion Lennox

June

NEW DOC IN TOWN	Meredith Webber
ORPHAN UNDER THE CHRISTMAS TREE	Meredith Webber
THE NIGHT BEFORE CHRISTMAS	Alison Roberts
ONCE A GOOD GIRL...	Wendy S. Marcus
SURGEON IN A WEDDING DRESS	Sue MacKay
THE BOY WHO MADE THEM LOVE AGAIN	Scarlet Wilson